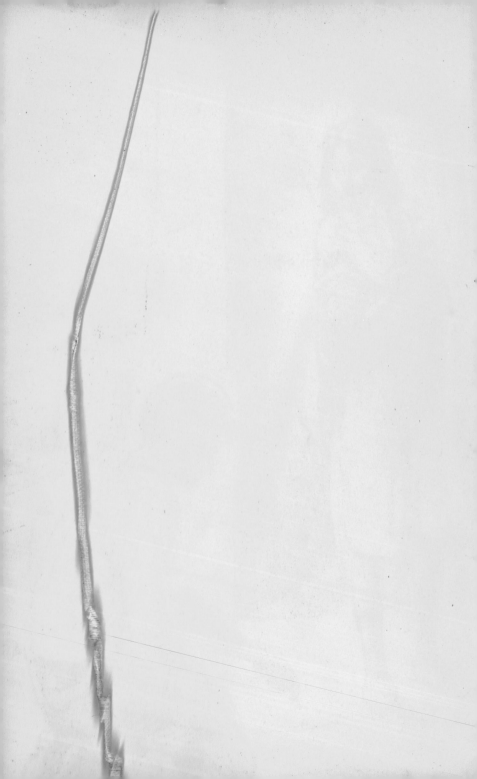

WHISPERING GIRL

Books by
FLORENCE CRANNELL MEANS

———

WHISPERING GIRL

a

Hopi Indian Story of Today

by Florence Crannell Means

illustrations by Oscar Howard

The Riverside Press Cambridge

HOUGHTON MIFFLIN COMPANY · BOSTON

The Riverside Press
CAMBRIDGE · MASSACHUSETTS
PRINTED IN THE U.S.A.

8406

TO CARL

For better, for worse, it could never have happened without you.

'Tawahonsi'

CONTENTS

1.   THE HOUSE ON TOP

THE stew was good. It was so good that the red-and-black
Hopi bowl on the floor was fast emptying. The girl Nuvensi
watched it through the screen of her lashes, measuring the
contents anxiously.

Hopis never gobbled their food. Nuvensi's foster-parents
ate with leisure and dignity, Father sitting on a stool two
inches high, Mother with feet turned sidewise on the adobe
floor in proper woman fashion. Foster-Brother, Nuvayesva,
was somewhat less polite. He did not gobble, but certainly
his ragged arm reached out often across Father's ragged
knee, dipping his roll of piki like a spoon into the common
dish.

Vensi and Nuva — they were nicknamed because their
clan names, Snowflake and Snow, were so similar — Vensi
and Nuva could seldom fill themselves to a comfortable
roundness. Always Vensi must decide which she should do:
hold in her mouth each separate morsel of mutton, each
big, round, succulent grain of hominy, each fat, golden
bean; or get all she could by eating straight along, as Nuva
did

Everything Mother's hands made, Vensi thought with a rush of affection, was better than anyone else's. Always Mother washed the hominy an extra time before putting it in with the meat: it was quite free from the bite of lye. Her piki you could tell from any other piki: the bundle of tissue, looking for all the world like the blue-gray paper of a hornet's nest, crackled with corn-rich goodness. Vensi hoped she could get one more dip in the stew with hers, but Nuva, with a deceptive look of deliberateness, bit off three more inches of his own piki, and then slowly scooped up the last of the meat with the end of the bundle.

Vensi captured the one remaining grain of hominy, giggling at her own disappointment. Father and Mother, who never seemed hungry themselves, smiled at their children. Nuva was gulping like a chicken that has tried to swallow too large a scrap, and he reached backward to ladle a drink of water out of the big pottery jar in the corner.

'Driving the sheep up to the corral, it makes a man empty from top to toe,' he excused himself, scowling and grinning at once.

That was Nuva. He could look as black as thunder, and then a smile would flash through his storm cloud like the summer sun. Vensi did not often stop to think about her foster-brother, but now, sucking the mutton juice from her hominy grain, to get all the good of it before she chewed and swallowed it, she observed him.

He looked enough like her to be her own brother, though they were no kin at all, not even clan kin, except by adoption. He was slim and straight, like a swift arrow: as slim as she, and no more than a few inches taller. But where his black mane was defiantly erect, her head drooped with her exceeding shyness. Like hers, his eyes were of so dense a brown as to look coal-black; and, like hers, they were large and lustrous. Like hers, too, they could lose themselves in their thick straight fringe of black lashes. It was their expression that differed: Nuva's blazed here, blazed there, unsmiling, taking in all there was to see without a turn of the head; while Vensi's glanced shyly from under lowered lids. Both noses were thin and aquiline; and the mouths were similar except that Nuva's lips curled scornfully and Vensi's wistfully. Both dark faces were tanned darker by the fierce sun: tanned to a smooth, clear brown, without spot or freckle. Nuva's hair, however, had kept its dense black, while Vensi's had warmed with brown lights.

Vensi thought, 'He is not big, but he would be good to look at — much better than I — if only he ever had decent clothes.'

Mother might have been thinking the same thoughts. 'A man,' she said, joking about Nuva's last remark, 'had better take the needle and thread and sew up his overalls before the light is gone. Like a wild Indian you look, all rags and tatters.'

Mother laughed while she said it, a high, soft laugh like the croon of a contented biddy. The words chirped and sang, too: the beautiful, correct Hopi which they all spoke when they were together.

A few minutes longer they sat still, mechanically clearing away every fragment, every crumb, that remained on the oilcloth spread before them on the adobe floor. Mother rubbed the end of her piki around and around the bowl to soften it with juice for the small Omva who leaned against her knees. Nuva gnawed for the third time a small bone from the stew, but unobtrusively, with good manners. Quiet and at ease and happy together were the five; and this was the hour that Vensi always treasured.

At this hour few callers came in through the low door; and Vensi was as shy of people as a desert rabbit or dove. She was not afraid of other things, but she was afraid of people: almost everyone outside this small, dear circle. Naturally she was most afraid of *bohannas*, white people;

but she was enough afraid of her own kind so that her voice
died in her throat when she must talk with them, and only a
whisper came from her mouth. So it had come about that
many called her the Whispering Girl.

Now the village was still except for a few comfortable
sounds that came up from below: children laughing inside
other houses, late sheep-bells clanking up to the corrals
that were cupped like giant stone swallows' nests under the
rim of the mesa. The room itself was shadowed with evening and at the same time ruddied and gilded with evening
sunshine. It was as if it floated in the sunset.

The village crowned the high mesa, and Mother's house
crowned the village — Mother's, because the Hopi house
always belongs to the woman. It was two ladders high.
Just below it was Tawamana's house. From Mother's
doorstep, on Tawamana's roof, one clambered down a ladder to Tawamana's doorstep, on Sikatsi's roof. Another
ladder led past Sikatsi's house-front to the solid rock of the
mesa top.

From where Vensi sat on the floor she could look out over
miles of desert. She looked through a glassless window a
foot square, which pierced the thick stone and adobe wall
above the grinding-bin and made an irregularly framed picture of sky and plain. Maybe Mother's ancestor had
peered through that peephole when she knelt to grind the
corn two hundred and fifty years ago, and watched with
fast-beating heart for wild Utes and Apaches, painted and
yelling on their ponies.

Today there was only the wide desert to see, and the
trader's car crossing it like a swift black beetle. That was
enough: the desert was itself a world. Trails meandered
over it like the thin scratches of a fingernail, the main road
a deeper scratch. Here and there its indeterminate color
seemed splashed with sunshine, each splash a sandy patch
where some Hopi had a field or fruit trees. At the edges

stood mesas that were stone in the middle of the day, but
now floating color as bright as flowers. And arching above
was a great smoking, blazing splendor of sky.

Even aside from its outlook, Mother's house was good.
Vensi did not think it so beautiful as that of Honawu's wife,
Lenmana. Vensi envied Lenmana her shiny oak china
closet and her shiny brass bed and her wood floor with its
linoleum rug. Yet here was a peace and quiet that filled
Vensi's eyes and heart.

Mother's house had two main rooms, at different levels,
separated from each other by three broad steps. The ceiling
poles had aged to a silver pallor, and — tied to the brush
that filled in between the poles — downy prayer-feathers
drifted in the breeze. Soft-toned floors and walls looked as
if loving hands had shaped every inch of them; and that
was true, for the adobe plaster was laid on with the bare
palm. This year Vensi had been old enough to do her share
of the spring plastering and whitewashing, and she noticed
the rightness of it more because she had had part in it. She
and Mother had warmed the white gypsum with red clay
till it had exactly the right flush of color.

There was little furniture to crowd and clutter the place
and rob it of its look of peace. There was a cookstove which
'Washindon' — the Government — had given them; a
loom where Father had a chief's blanket half woven; a pole
for 'soft goods,' hanging like a long trapeze from the ceiling;
a roll of sheepskins and quilts which were spread on the
floor for beds at night; the grinding-bin, set into the adobe
floor, its three graduated millstones at an angle like wash-
boards.

That was all the furniture. But the setting sun shone on
the walls, lighting strings of red chillies and the year's last
festoons of dried beans, a few richly woven basket trays
from this mesa and from Oraibi, a few gaily painted wooden
katchina dolls. And because this was the House on Top,

and because the peephole and a larger glassless window were always open, and usually the door also, the breeze blew sweetly through higher room and lower room.

No long strings of handwrought silver beads and squash-blossoms hung from the pegs driven between the stones; no belts with heavy silver *conchos*; no brilliantly striped Pendleton blankets. The Family had such treasures, but they were hanging in the trader's wide-open safe or in his cupboard, with other pawned goods. Even Vensi's modest store of silver and turquoise bracelets and rings; even Nuva's ring and bow-guard, had traveled to the trader's and stayed there.

For a little while this winter there had been a wealth of fluffy new sheepskins for beds. That was because a heavy snow had caught Father off guard, and six sheep had piled up for shelter and had been smothered. The skins were all Father could salvage, and they were so clean and so well cured that tourists offered him a dollar apiece for them. Six dollars was a sum to be grasped without delay. It was maybe a tenth of all the cash money Father and Mother would handle in a year.

Yes, the House on Top was a shabby place; but it was clean and well ordered, and it had a river of air flowing through it, sweet and cool, on the hottest, most reeking days. Besides, Father and Mother had made it home.

Vensi did not need to look at them to find the reason; but she did look, contentedly. Father sat lightly clasping his moccasined ankles in strong brown hands. From chin to ankles Father was common blue denim, worn and washed almost white. But his moccasins, though shabby, were right Hopi, well made and trim; his glossy black hair, cut even with his neck at the sides and wrapped in a knot behind, was jauntily bound round the brow with a red kerchief; and big sky-blue turquoises swung from his ears. Father's mouth and eyes looked always as if about to smile, and the lines of his face were shaped by a deep and gentle kindliness. When Omva staggered over to him, her uncertain baby feet set wide, and gripped him by the nose to keep from falling, Father's smile-lines deepened.

He said, 'Big Sister has given you a happy day, I think, now that her school is done.'

Indeed, Vensi's back ached with that giving. She had slung Omva on her shoulders in her shawl and carried her everywhere she went; to the spring, after brush, and to Grandmother's to borrow baking-powder.

Mother said, 'It is good to have them home from school.'

Mother's face was as kind as Father's. It was a strong face, beaten by the high winds and burned by the desert sun and thinned by hunger. Like a carving it was set between the wings of black hair that ended in long coils over her shoulders. Perhaps it was the eyes that made it still a beautiful face: they were of a clear hazel, and fringed with lashes heavy like a girl's.

Father asked, 'Are the boy and girl glad to be free from school, I wonder?'

Nuva tossed his stormy mane. 'Yes. Why not? I would rather herd sheep all day — alone, even — than be shut into a tight room to study stupid *bohanna* matters.... Except for the paints one can use at school, and the good paper,' he added, his tone changing.

'And our daughter?' Father went on gently.

Vensi flushed and, without meaning to, glanced down her patched, outgrown dress to her toes, which were poking through her shoes.

'I know,' Mother said quickly. 'You need new clothes. In school you were ashamed. Perhaps your father and Nuva can find time from the flock and the fields to work at the school and earn your clothes. Or perhaps if the wool sells better, and then if we can sell the young mutton well ——'

'If there should be more rain this summer, so that the corn and beans are not burned out, and the peaches ——'
Father agreed.

'And if Honawu ——' Mother added.

That was it: most of the Family's troubles came back to Honawu. If Honawu would not press that gambling debt — for Father did sometimes gamble, good as he was in every other way — if Honawu would not take sly advantage of Father at every turn — if Honawu would not rouse the Village Council to enmity against Father ——

Honawu's girl, Polemana, had fresh new dresses from the mail-order catalogue, and shiny shoes, and a coat when she wanted a coat, and a fine striped Pendleton when she wanted a blanket. Honawu always had plenty, even after a hard winter or a dry summer, though certainly he did not work overmuch at his trade of carpentry.

In short, Honawu's very name broke this sweet, close tranquillity. It brought in envy. It brought unease.

Yes, this house had a rightness, an order, that was beauty; and Mother was one of the best basket-makers on the Reservation, and one of the best cooks. Father had good fields, drawn from the community lands, and he worked hard in them. He had a flock of sheep, and he did not neglect it. He was a skilful weaver, besides. The Family should have prospered; yet at every turn they ran into difficulties.

Honawu offered explanations for the difficulties, and so did Mutz, his clan-brother and crony. Sometimes they said it was because Mother had been too friendly to the Mission. Bad fortune followed Hopis who went astray after strange religions. For instance: long ago one of the columns of Corn Rock, on the shoulder of this mesa, had crumbled into the plain because Hopis had been having traffic with white gods; and thereupon had followed a famine which came near wiping out the tribe, and forced fathers and

mothers to sell their children to the Mexicans for corn on
which to live. And for another instance: Awatobi, a sister
village, had welcomed the long-coats, the padres, and see
what had happened: for two hundred and fifty years now
Awatobi had lain a crushed and smoke-blackened ruin.

Mother's suspected leanings were more serious because
she was of a Valuable Family. In a room that lay hidden
between the floor of this higher room and the ceiling of
Tawamana's, stood the Old, Precious Things of Mother's
clan. At set times she carried corn meal to feed them, and
piki and hominy; and thither on certain days came her
brothers to make prayers before them.

The children were not supposed to see these precious
objects, but they had seen them: a stone lion-dog, very
ancient, with one eye of turquoise and one of cannel coal;
and other fetishes, somewhat resembling creatures, and
somewhat resembling stones that had lain long in a stream
of water. There stood lightning-sticks, too, twisted and
writhing like angular snakes. It was said that all these
things had been brought up from the Underworld by the
first clan members, back in the dimness of the past, before
the long-coats; before ever the Spanish had come with their
glistening metal bodies set on the monstrous beasts that had
been the first horses on the continent.

Because of her responsibility for these Old, Precious
Things, Mother needed to be especially careful that her
actions were pleasing to the gods, said Honawu.

At other times he said it was Father who brought the ill-
luck by his kindness to the whites. As a matter of fact,
Father had no traffic with the Mission, nor did he find most
of the whites likable; but he would not harm them or harass
them; and Honawu declared that what the tribe needed
was Hopis who were Hopis through and through.

Yet again Honawu and Mutz would give a different explanation: that the bearers of ill-fortune were not so much

Father and Mother — Yoki and Sivenka — as their foster-children. Nuva and Vensi had heard those whispers. It was the consciousness of them, maybe, that made Nuva so proud and angry and Vensi so shy. In a place like Middle Village, where a hundred and fifty people were crowded together on the crown of the mesa, a boy and girl could be mightily unhappy over what a hundred and forty are saying about them; mightily unhappy over being creatures by some mystery set apart from the world.

All this thinking had not taken Vensi long: only long enough for Mother's softly singing voice to say: 'Yet maybe we are wrong to complain, "If Honawu this," and "If Honawu that." I think it is not men who set our ways. Likewise, if we wish food and clothing and health, and if we wish our prayers to be strong, then we must look to it that our feet follow clean paths.'

Father nodded slowly, but Nuva grumbled under his breath.

'Honawu's feet — are they in clean paths?' he demanded. 'Yet I should think Honawu gets what he wants.'

'Shhh!' Mother cautioned. 'Someone comes.'

The door opened. On the threshold in the soft gray twilight a boy of Nuva's age stood breathless.

'Where do you come from, my young friend?' Father asked in the Hopi words of formal greeting.

'I come from Mees McClung,' the boy answered. Edging inside, he squatted on his heels and waited.

'Did the Mission-Mary send some word to us?' Mother inquired, after a meditative silence. . . . Strange that one after another the workers at the Mission should each be named Mission-Mary; but so it was.

'Yes. On her doorstep, wrapped in a flour sack, a *tiposie*, a baby, very small.'

Mother clucked anxiously.

'Mees McClung cannot make that baby eat.'

Again Mother clucked.

'She says, Will Sivenka come and show her?'

'Tonight?' asked Mother Sivenka.

'Or it will die,' the boy assented.

'We come,' said Mother.

Her voice sounded strained. Her eyes had passed the boy's face; with dislike and dread they rested on another, which peered over his head. Vensi's glance followed hers. The new face was small and deeply lined, and it topped a crooked and spidery body. There was malice in the narrow eyes, bright as black beetles' wings, and in the voice that drawled sneeringly:

'You will be wise not to add another *tiposie* to your flock. These you already have, they look thin as if fed on corn husks. The new Agent is likely to take them from you and give them to one who can fatten them. Even the Village Council talks of appointing a new guardian. Such is their right.'

Vensi's heart plunged sickly and she shot a stricken glance at Father and Mother. Their mouths were tight. No one answered Honawu; unless Mother's wordless murmur was answer. It was a manners-murmur, deep in her throat.

'Nuva and I will go with the women,' Father said quietly. 'We may as well. Thus we can bring home water from Lemova Spring.'

WITHOUT more words, the Family made ready for the walk down the mesa.

Father and Nuva brought water-cans from the storeroom and then went out to find the hobbled burros. But first they paused to make themselves more presentable, ladling water from the jar in the corner and rubbing their hands and faces with it.

As for Mother and Vensi, they flew. Mother jerked another dress, ragged but clean, on Omva, who resisted by sitting down and making herself limp. Not discouraged, Mother washed the child's face and hands and snatched up the handleless broom and brushed her hair smartly with the hairbrush end of it. Then she took another look and dusted off Omva's brown little legs and feet where they showed below her long dress. At this last indignity Omva's patience gave out with a yell. Mother did not let her have her own way, as she usually did. No, she finished the dusting; for white people, even the nicest, like Miss McClung, seldom took into account the adobe floors and their way of powdering little bodies till they looked like floured molasses cookies.

Vensi brushed her own hair with hard slaps of the broom, and washed herself; but she had no better dress to change to, so she folded her shawl concealingly around herself. Mother slipped on her last Christmas apron, gift of the Mission, and then deftly scooped Omva up on her back and secured her there in the folds of her blanket.

'The rubber nipples,' she told Vensi; 'I have kept them tied up in a rag yonder. Mees McClung will have bottles, I think.'

'Only one nipple,' Vensi reported, when she had climbed on a stool and clawed the rag-wrapped object out of a crevice.

'Yes, I remember. Omva bit the end off one, and the other she lost over the edge of the mesa,' Mother recalled.

She padlocked the door, and she and Vensi clambered swiftly down the two ladders to the street. The men were not in sight. They had tired of waiting and gone on.

Honawu's daughter, Polemana, called to Vensi from her doorway, next to the house of Sikatsi; and Sikatsi's girl, just smaller than Vensi, ran out and walked with them, hopping first on one foot, then on the other. At the top of the trail Mother told the child to turn back: Hopi girls were not supposed to run about alone in the evening.

Father and Nuva were only a little way ahead, jogging along behind the two burros. The walk was a pleasant one in the twilight. The sky had cooled to violet and primrose and faint blue, and over east of First Mesa the moon came

up, big and pale and lovely. Though Vensi's heart was still
shaken by Honawu's words, it swelled with an irresistible
joy in the sweet night and in her oneness with the Family.

Their way passed in sight of the Government Day School.
Amid the cliffs of the mesa it sat back in a thick shade of
cottonwoods, all the little new leaves rustling with a sound
of rain.

'The nurse's house is black. No light,' said Mother.

Vensi thought that the field nurse was doubtless out on
a long trip, else Miss McClung would have telephoned her
for advice about this baby, instead of sending to the Top
for Mother.

Presently their trail bent around Corn Rock and the
cemetery above it, where planting-sticks protruded from
the men's graves and brooms from the women's, and pottery bowls and prayer-sticks and other objects clustered
around the lonely heaps of stone. Vensi, who all her life had
seen Corn Rock without thinking much about it, remembered suddenly the old tales of the famine, and how fathers
and mothers, weeping, had brought their children to this
broken column and bartered them for corn that would keep
life a little while in their other children. Vensi thought,
*How did those little bags of bones feel, carried from home and
from their mothers?* — and she pressed closer to Mother, so
that she could feel the comforting strength of her body.

Next the trail led past Lemova Spring, a sacred place and
precious. Father and Nuva were waiting for them there,
though they would not fill the water-cans until the return
trip. Father was looking to a high screen of brush woven
round a tree near the spring. It was Father's own apricot
tree, and he had to keep it protected from burros and goats
and, if possible, from boys. Vensi could see by the moonlight that the fruit was well advanced in that sheltered
place. Her mouth watered for its sweet and sour. The
Family's store of melons and dried peaches had been used

up by early spring, and canned peaches and oranges from the trading-post — and canned tomatoes, that luscious delicacy — were out of the question for the Family's purse.

Soon, though, there would be young onions to vary their diet, for two of the small terraced patches below the spring were theirs. Those plots were hardly bigger than the teacher's desk at school, but every inch of them was used, and one was well fringed with dark green onion tops. For here the spring was so near that there was plenty of water for the succulent plants.

On down the trail they swung, and out among the tumbled hillocks at the foot of the mesa: numberless sandy hillocks, as if the mesa had spilled them, helterskelter, out of its lap. The small stone houses and the small stone church looked like fragments of mesa and plain, except that, from the Mission, lights were shining in pale yellow oblongs. Nuva hobbled the burros again, tying their forefeet together with strips of rag so that they could not wander far. The Family stood at the Mission door.

When it opened, Vensi stumbled over the threshold after the others. The Mission was terribly bright. For several years now these night-time suns had dangled by long ropes from the ceilings, but Vensi had not yet lost her awe of them. Nuva had explained to her that they held no magic except *bohanna* magic, made with machines. He himself had been down in the Mission cellar and had seen the Delco plant that chugged away, noisily bringing the 'medicine.' Perhaps it brought it from the Underworld; or perhaps, since the *bohannas* did not seem to favor the Underworld, this magic came from above.

The Hopis, Nuva said, made rain by means of the Snake Dance, and the Mission-Mary made sunshine by means of *bohanna* machines. However that was, it shone almost blindingly after the dim oil lamps or the firelight in the House on Top. It not only dazzled Vensi's eyes: it mud-

dled her heart and mind. The whites were such strange
people. Most of them were ugly and ill-mannered; few of
them knew how to do the commonest of the needful things
of life; yet the sun and the moon bowed down to them;
earth gave them choice gifts — water, food, light — without labor; storm and cold could seldom come at them, nor
the hot sun parch them. So maybe it was not strange that
they were proud, thinking the Hopis unworthy beings, and
laughable. Seldom did a Mission-Mary behave so: the
Mission-Marys said that they were all God's creatures, and
they acted accordingly. Yet even the Mission-Marys were
whites, and thus a queer people, past understanding.

Vensi and Nuva sat on a couch in the corner and Father
and Mother on chairs that Miss McClung pushed out from
the dining-table for them. The boy and girl were used to
chairs, since they had spent eight or more years in school;
and Father had a high seat in his wagon; but Mother was
ill at ease when she must sit up in the air: she said her feet
went to sleep.

Since Miss McClung knew a good deal of Hopi and Father some English, those two exchanged commonplaces of
conversation, while the young people looked stealthily
around the room. Against one wall stood the piano, which
Vensi longed to be left alone with, and beside it the telephone, another piece of *bohanna* magic which had grown
common to their eyes, though neither of them had ever
talked through one. Nuva was feeling the linoleum-covered
floor thoughtfully with his broken shoe. There it was, also
a *bohanna* triumph, smooth and bright and with no dust to
come off on everything that touched it. Honawu's wife had
some of it for her best room, and so did a few others of Middle Village; but for most Hopis it cost too much.

The thoughts of the four Hopis went on weaving a shadowy skein in the brightness, with little Omva probably not
thinking much, but clinging tight to Mother and stealing

quick shining glances at Miss McClung. And then the silence was broken by a thin wail from the next room. It was like the mew of a kitten too young to have its eyes open. It sounded almost indifferent, as if mildly fretting at having to stay, and it died away in sighing whimpers.

Mother started from her chair as if someone had pricked her. She and Miss McClung collided in the bedroom doorway, and Mother pushed on into the room ahead of the white woman, her boldness showing how deep a baby's cry could pierce.

She came out with Omva fretting at her skirts and a tiny bundle held against her breast. She looked across it at Father, and her eyebrows rose to a pitiful peak on her forehead, and her mouth drew downward. Father and Vensi came softly and peered at the foundling.

'*Okiway*, alas!' mourned Mother. 'The poor *tiposhoya*, little baby. Did you ever see a smaller?'

Vensi's heart gave a great leap of pity and surprise. Pity, because this baby's head was no bigger than Vensi's small brown fist, its hands bird-claws, its eyes large and solemn in the pinched tininess of its face. Surprise, because the thick fur which covered its little head was not black but as creamy white as wild oats rising out of an autumn snow. The baby's skin was the snow; or maybe it was an almond blossom; and its eyes were the strangest blue, like the sky between daylight and dark.

'Is it *bohanna*?' Father inquired. 'Or — not?'

'Not' — Miss McClung shook her head from side to side as she said it. 'Not *bohanna*. Another albino Hopi. From Hotevilla, maybe: he was laid on a basket of Oraibi reeds, like an offering here on my doorstep, and a whisper has come to me that his parents were Hotevilla. He had not been bathed. I do not think he had been given food or water. That is another whisper that I have heard. Not water! As if it were not sorrow enough for him that his

mother went out of the world when he came in, poor inno-
cent little flower. I can't understand them; no, I cannot.'

Some of this she said in Hopi and some in English. It did
not matter what language she spoke, for Father and Mother
were not listening. Father stared at the baby, and the lines
around his mouth deepened with stern kindliness.

Vensi's lip dropped. 'Why, a baby couldn't live,' she
whispered. 'Why, even a kitten I once found ——'

'This one has lived,' Miss McClung said with gloomy
triumph. 'But it won't keep on living if we can't get it to
eat. . . . Sivenka, I tried a medicine-dropper and almost
choked him. They say the nurse was called to Five Houses.
I don't know what's wrong out there, but she hasn't come
back, and I didn't know what to do next. You have such
good luck, Sivenka.'

'There are canned milk and corn syrup?' Mother asked.
'Vensi, you take the baby — carefully! — and hold him as
I am holding him. I fix the milk as the field nurse showed
me when you yourself were small and frail.'

Timidly Vensi followed the women into the kitchen.
While Mother opened cans and mixed and tasted; while
Miss McClung lighted the unseen fuel in the stove and
pointed out small bottles that already stood on their heads
in hot water, Vensi gazed down into that morsel of a face;
into those eyes that looked nowhere with a sort of distant
anger and majesty, as if there were nothing worth seeing.

It was not even a weight on Vensi's thin arms: it was only
a frail warmth, like a petal on which the sun has shone.
There seemed small chance that the petal could survive the
world's cold and heat. If it had been an ordinary baby and
had died, Vensi well knew what would have happened: how
it would have been wrapped in a blanket and carried out by
its father and thrust deep into one of the crevices in the flat
rock that stretched like a floor behind the village. Food
would have been set there for the small soul, and the father

would have traced a corn meal path back to the mother's house, so that the baby spirit could have found its way home. Because such a tiny soul, weak and small and knowing nothing — how could it harm the living as an older spirit might?

Thus would it have happened with a common baby, but this was no common baby. This was a witch-baby, an evil spirit cloaked in sweet childish flesh and bringing death to its mother. It had no right to live, and if it died it had no right to come home again. In the old days such a one was buried with the mother; and there was not much cruelty in that punishment, for death came to the little one almost before it had found life. Nowadays, though, 'Washindon' disapproved of such action; so the matter was handled otherwise. Sometimes, it was said, the evil little creature was left untended in a forgotten corner. But others said No, a kindly relative carried it to the Mission-Mary or to some other *bohanna* doorstep, and then, if it lived, it would not bring misfortune to the village from which it had been cast out. If it died —— But this little almond-blossom was one of those who clung stubbornly to life.

There were many reasons why a tear splashed out of Vensi's eye. The tear plopped down on the infinitely small mouth of the boy-baby, opening to mew again. Mother was turning about with the bottle, whose heat she had been testing by shaking a drop on the inside of her wrist. As she turned, the tear splashed and the baby's lips closed and its fragile throat moved in an infinitesimal swallow.

'*Lolama*, good!' crowed Mother, and with care she pressed his pointed chin with one forefinger, while she shook a drop of milk into the laxly opening mouth.

A half-hour later the foundling had taken a full teaspoon of milk and lay asleep against Mother's breast, his fingers half-curled, like wilted blossoms, and his transparent lids almost closed over the blue darkness of his eyes.

'By your teas you have saved him,' Mother said proudly to Vensi.

'He was probably just ready to give up and swallow anyway,' Miss McClung said practically. For the first time she settled back in her rocking-chair, though she did not yet loosen the wires that strung her body so tight, but clasped the chair arms convulsively and swung rapidly to and fro as if on a rocking-horse. 'But now — what had I best do with him, I wonder? I'd like to keep him myself, I surely would. But I've already too much on my hands.'

'He needs mothering,' Mother said thoughtfully.

'Maybe I could persuade Sehepmana to take him, once he seems to be started,' Miss McClung thought aloud.

Mother's brows knitted. 'In Sehepmana's house is much breathing-sickness, and the *bohannas* say ——'

'T.B. Truly,' agreed Miss McClung, nodding her head a great many times, and patting her foot on the floor with each nod. 'Perhaps then Kabuser ——'

'Kabuser,' Mother argued, 'has been so long without babies in the house. She would not remember their little needs. When Omva came to us, we had to learn all over again, because Vensi was already fourteen.'

Miss McClung burst out laughing. She brought her rocker to an abrupt halt and leveled a forefinger at Mother. 'You want this baby yourself!' she accused her. 'That's why you make so many objections.'

In surprise Mother looked from the baby to Miss McClung, and then she, too, began to laugh. But she quickly sobered.

'How should we want another baby?' she protested. 'Even as it is, some are saying in the village that the new Agent will take these three from us and give them to one who can better fatten them. Or even that the Village Council may do so, because they are orphans and the village has a right to choose the guardians for orphans. And certainly

we are far from rich. Last winter the heavy   .ows, and our
horses leaping from the cliff corral ——'

Vensi studied the stocking toe which protruded from the
gray-worn tip of her shoe. The stocking had been darned
until it made holes in her feet, but her toe was peeping
through the darns again. She sighed. If they took this
baby, and must buy canned milk for it, and Karo, Father
and Nuva would have to work so hard to earn the food that
they could not possibly get time to earn clothing, too. She
must go ill-shod to school, or wear moccasins, which none
of the school-children did. She would never have anything;
never get her silver bracelets back from pawn; never get a
bright new dress out of the catalogue. She looked at the
baby, and Nuva's eyes met hers there. She knew what
Nuva must be thinking: of clothes, too, for he liked to look
trig and dashing; but more of pencils and paint and paper.

Nuva's fingers were always itching to make pictures: the
ancient symbolic figures that his people loved; the elaborate
color and movement of the ceremonies; the villages set like
lighted ivory in the turquoise sky. Only last spring his
teacher had sent to a contest in a far city Nuva's painting
of the sacred plants, corn and tobacco and melon and bean,
shining against the blue sky.

To a contest of National Youth his teacher had sent it,
where boys and girls all over the land were entering their
pictures, in hope of the magnificent prizes. If Nuva could
win the thousand-dollar first prize, Vensi had said —— But
Nuva said he could not imagine what a person would do
with a thousand dollars. A thousand dollars was too much,
like a bad dream you might have when you had eaten the
magic green beans at the Midwinter Festival. But if he
were to win the smallest prize of all, five dollars, he knew
what he would do: spend it for thick paper and good brushes
and smooth paint. Really, he said, he would rather win the
five dollars.

Yet in spite of all these considerations Vensi and Nuva were the last people in the world who should oppose the adoption of this snow-blossom. And, besides, it might be a sent saying, that of Mother's, 'By your tears you have saved him.' What you have saved you must cherish.

Vensi swallowed hard, because it was so painful to speak before any outsider. 'Fatness is not everything,' she whispered, 'and so small a one will not eat much.'

(No, not much: only new dresses and shoes and paints and brushes.)

The Mission-Mary had stopped rocking and tapping her foot, and the whole room had quieted to hear Vensi, being used to her frightened whisper. Father's smile-brackets deepened to tenderness as he looked at her.

To Nuva his glance moved on. 'And you, my son?'

Nuva scuffed his broken shoes on the linoleum and scowled. His big black eyes flashed sidewise at Father, and his mouth looked angry. 'Even a lost lamb you would pick up and carry home, I should think,' he said crossly.

Mother crowed high with laughter. 'I hadn't known what was wrong with us,' she said to Miss McClung. 'We have grown so solemn' — she pulled a long and doleful face — 'and so dull. We needed a baby. Nothing is so dear as a baby. And see, Small Sister is already a big girl. Practically grown.'

They all laughed at that. Omva was a round little Cloud, but small for even her eighteen or twenty months. She looked like a doll walking as she pattered across the room with her wide-legged baby waddle. She leaned against Mother's knees and poked the small bundle on Mother's breast with a tiny brown finger.

'*Lo'ma*, pitty!' she said gravely.

'You see!' said Father. 'Talking. A grown woman indeed.'

'Well, then, there's clothes to think of,' Miss McClung

declared briskly. 'I have some pretty ones that were sent by the churches. Vensi, suppose you come and help me.'

Her voice trailed after her as she pattered up the boxed-in stairway, and Vensi tiptoed behind to the storeroom under the eaves.

There she looked around her curiously. Boxes and barrels were stacked solidly with aisles between, each container labeled in careful lettering. Miss McClung opened one marked 'Layettes,' and while Vensi was spelling out the strange word to herself and wondering what it could possibly mean, the Mission-Mary lifted out white little shirts and soft gowns edged with blue and pink and a tall stack of diapers. She piled them across Vensi's arms and added two thick, soft, woolly blankets, pink and blue.

Vensi drew a deep breath. '*Eskwalli*, thank you,' she whispered, and followed Miss McClung down and stood silent before her mother with the pile of baby clothes on her outstretched arms.

Mother said, '*Eskwalli — lolama — eskwalli!*' ducking her head and smiling with pleasure. Father tiptoed over and looked at the bright little garments and murmured, '*Quaequae*, thank you, my friend.' His word was different, because in Hopi some words have man-forms and woman-forms. 'Thank you' is one of these.

Mother wrapped the new baby carefully. Miss McClung put the clothes in a box, with the bottles and six cans of milk and one of Karo to get the Family started, and Nuva took the box without comment. Father lifted Omva to Vensi's back, and she folded her shawl around the child and herself. Mother carried the new baby against her breast under her blanket, where no cool breath of air could chill it. They went out into the moonlight.

The hobbled burros were jouncing up a near slope, their cans clinking as they grazed on the scanty clumps of salt-weed. Nuva set down his box and ran lithely to catch them.

'We came five, we go six,' Father said softly, when they were on their way once more.

Now that the moon was high, the trail was even more beautiful. Below, in the dry wash, the early corn could be clearly seen, planted in painstaking terraces edged with brush, to catch the first trickle of water. Piles of stones stood beside them, watchmen to guard the tiny fields while their owners were 'On Top.' The stair-step gardens of Lemova Spring were painted bright white and black by the pure light, and the spring itself, within its deep stone walls, was dark with mystery. As Father and Nuva unlashed their cans, a strange, wild cry sounded from somewhere — whether from apricot tree or hanging gardens or pool they could not tell — a call clear with beauty and echoing eerily through the quiet night. Vensi thought she had never known a moment so perfect.

Yet a shadow fell across the bright path of the Family as they trudged around the corner at the top of the trail. It was a long shadow, though the thing that cast it was so small and crooked — Honawu, lounging before his house door as if awaiting them.

'Again!' he commented sourly. 'Again!'

'*Antsa*, truly,' Foster Father agreed as he lifted the full water-cans from his burro.

Yes, again. For, some sixteen years ago, Father and Mother had found on their doorstep a neglected bundle of boy-babyhood. They had taken him into their house, lonesome for the children who had come to them early in their marriage, only to go quickly away into the dark. A little later, in far Hotevilla, Father had chanced upon a girl-baby in a deep basket of meal where she lay whimpering out a shaken cry of protest against the world. The girl-baby and the boy-baby were Nuva and Vensi. Vensi was a year old before Father and Mother learned for certain the terrifying truth: that these both were witch-babies, dangerous to the

tribe and to their protectors. But by that time Nuva's
stormy baby eyes, his stormy knitted brow, his sturdy in-
dependence, had bound Father and Mother to him with
ties stronger than fear; and little Vensi's timid baby sweetness, her wide-eyed gentleness, had won all their love.

Eighteen months or two years ago, Mother had fetched
the motherless Omva home from the Government hospital
at the Canyon, where she had been left unclaimed after her
mother's death. Father and Mother were perhaps the first
Hopis ever to dare so greatly.

Small wonder, then, that Nuva and Vensi could not close
the door against this strange, pale-haired waif. His lot had
been theirs, also. Like him, they were held to be the dwell-
ing-places of evil spirits, who had brought death when they
received life.

Yes, again Father and Mother had brought into the village an unlucky being.

Up the ladders climbed the Family, out from under the
crooked shadow and into the haven of home. The door they
left wide to catch all the moonlight, for there was no oil in
the lamps.

By that white moonlight and the flicker of a fire which
Vensi kindled on the hearth in the corner, they made ready
for bed, and Mother laid herself upon the sheepskin with
the new baby warm upon her own body.

It was more richly home than ever, because of the new
one who was come into it.

WHEN dawn came into
the House on Top, Vensi
brought the cradle from the storeroom.
There, for months, it had hung among
odds and ends: fox skins, for the ceremonies, twig caps with gourds for horns, and
the like.

The cradle was of basketwork, its end
curved upward in a lovely line to meet the
bow. Mother made a soft bed of clean cloths
upon it and laid the tiny baby there. She
spread the new blankets over him, up to his
shoulders, and laced the cords across as if she
were lacing a foot into a shoe. Indeed, the
cradle was like a great willow sandal, only
with the toe strap at center instead of side.

'It is best, I think,' Mother said thoughtfully, 'not
to move him, not to handle him, more than need be.

He has so little
strength, so little blood.   It is all he can do just to draw
breath and keep the life coursing through his pale body.'

She put him on a pile of sheepskins in a corner behind the
stove, where no drafts came to break the even warmth.
Also she threw a quilt over the cradle-bow, so that the
tiposhoya lay grandly in his own little tent. When the
people of the village came climbing the ladders to see this
new one, Mother or Vensi lifted no more than a corner of
the quilt, and let the guests look and wonder without dis-
turbance to the small being.

Omva was a problem. Every five minutes she staggered
around behind the stove, murmuring, 'Hot! Hot!' remind-
ingly to herself, and then crowing with delight as she poked
her round little face in beside this soft, warm doll.

Again and again Vensi sprang trembling to the rescue.
'If she should fall against him!' she murmured. 'Mother,
she was feeling the soft top, where his head breathes!'

Again and again, patiently, Mother told Omva: 'No, no!
the *tiposhoya* might be hurt! Gently, Little Sister.'

And again and again Omva could be heard warning herself: 'Gently, Little Sister! Mustn't touch!' and shaking her
small head sternly, even while she crept in beneath the boy-
baby's canopy.

'Mees McClung says a spank really does no harm and
much good,' Vensi declared when for the dozenth time she
had shaken the corn meal from her hands and lifted Omva
out of the tempting corner.

'Mees McClung is good, and often she is also right,'
Mother called up from the storeroom, wiping the sweat from
her forehead with the curve of her elbow so that it should not
drip on the piki she was baking. 'But Hopis do not beat
their children. That you know well. Children — they are
far too precious.'

'A spank is not a beating,' Vensi persisted under her
breath. But she knew it was no use urging Mother to spank,
however busy they might be, and however troublesome the
little Omva.

The Family was busier than usual. The bean-planting
was already overdue, and now it must wait no longer. The
beans and the early sweet corn were in acres four miles
away, near the Family's small ranch-house, and they
would all go and settle there for a while.

All day they labored over their preparations. Vensi
knelt to grind the corn, singing softly as she scrubbed the
'sons-of-millstones,' like flat lava rolling-pins, up and down
the slanting millstones. She made great panfuls of the flour-
soft meal, straightening her tired back only to leap protect-
ingly to the baby's cradle or to brush the stones clear of
meal with a broom-grass brush, so that they would again
bite strongly. Mother used some of the meal to make piki,
for wherever they went they took piki. Grinding, piki-
making, both used all the joints and muscles of a woman's
body.

Early the next morning they packed into their wagon the
supplies they would need, and Nuva and Vensi carried up
from the corral four lambs too new and feeble to follow the
flock, and three curled little kids. Then Vensi ran and
watched Father and Nuva catch the gray mules, there in
the village corral.

The corral was only a broad shelf of rock, five feet below
the level of the village street. It needed no wall, nor any
fence, for its outer edge was the rim of a precipice that
plunged down a hundred feet to the ledge. Seldom did an
animal fall over that rim. Yet last year Father's team of
horses had fallen. It had been mysterious, that fall; but
Honawu explained it easily: it had happened because
Mother had gone to sewing-meeting at the Mission the day
before.

Mules were wiser than horses, anyway, Father said; and
these mules were especially wise and especially nimble:
small, trim gray beasts with twinkling little black hoofs.

It was Nuva's task to herd the flock across the four miles

of desert. Before the rest of the Family had settled itself in
the wagon, he had set out, a bundle of bread and a mutton
bone wrapped in a bandanna in his hand, and Askee, the
family dog, leaping and barking around the pattering feet
of the flock. The sun had climbed only a finger's breadth
above the horizon when boy and dog had to herd the woolly
creatures out among the rocks and leave the road clear for
the mules to tick past, the Family grinning at the boy beneath the rolled up canvas of the wagon-cover.

This was another fine time of day. In the level rays of
light the mesas were again melting into something quite
different from rocks and cactus: shapes of stone, but colors
of flowers, red and violet and yellow.

Mother sat in the bed of the wagon, the *tiposhoya's* small
tent between her knees and Omva crowded possessively
against her. Vensi perched on the high spring seat beside
Father, Nuva's place when he was with them. It was
pleasant there, for the fresh goodness of the morning
streamed through her thin clothing and, besides, she could
see everything as the light wagon spun along.

Not that there were many things to see, in the four-mile
ride. With his rope-and-stick whip Father pointed to a
dark speck in the sky above Hukatuwi, Flat-Topped Butte.
Hukatuwi 'belonged' to Uyi, oldest man of his clan. That is
to say, his were the eagles that nested there, and every
spring, old as he was, he climbed its craggy sides, fought
off the parent birds, and carried home the young ones. On
his housetop he chained them until time for the stately
death which would free their eagle spirits to carry messages
to the gods. Father looked covetously at that wheeling
speck. Eagles were scarce this year and he had not been so
fortunate as to secure any, though he, too, was a clan head,
and should wing prayers to the Mighty.

Once or twice Vensi jumped off the high seat and ran
along behind the wagon to stretch her cramped legs. It

was fun to look for the tracks of beetles in sandy parts of the road: they traced a delicate braided pattern as they went. She located some fine clusters of pale purple blossoms, in rounded star-shapes; she would remember where they grew, and would gather the seeds when they formed, and Mother would grind them and mix them with canned milk to spread on bread for a treat. She picked a few thrifty stalks of Indian tobacco for Father's cigarettes, and a handful of a cool-looking plant with green leaves and white stems and blossoms. Mother used it to drive out the chicken-bugs that bit so hard. Nor did Vensi miss any scrap of brush for the fire, though she was careful never to reach into a clump of herbage without first making sure that it concealed no muscular spangled rattlesnake or deadly small sidewinder.

The only habitations they passed were the five houses of Five Houses, drifted deep in sand, and one Navajo hut. It was the summer hogan, a mere circle of brush built with a tree as its living pillar, and roofed with the tree's sparse branches. Father eased his team to a walk and waved a hand toward the men lounging there in the sun. In general Hopis and Navajos were hereditary enemies; but these particular Navajos were friendly people; and, besides, the man was a brother, for he was of the Navajo Snow Clan, and Father of the same order among the Hopis.

A quarter-mile farther on, Father stopped and Mother built a small fire of greasewood and warmed a bottle for the *tiposhoya*, who was much too small to be kept waiting. When the baby had milk, Omva must have something, too. She had an eye to the bottle, which she vaguely remembered as a delight of her past; but Mother distracted her with a lump of skillet-bread. The sight of her tiny teeth set in the fried bread made Vensi's mouth water and her stomach go sharp with emptiness. She was glad to be diverted by the approach of a slow-moving flock.

At its edge walked the shepherdess, a small erect figure whom Vensi recognized with a shy wave of her hand. This was Dezba, daughter of the hogan they had lately passed. She, like Vensi and Nuva, went to Lemova Day School, since her winter hogan was within horseback distance of it in good weather. This camp Dezba was very unlike the school Dezba. At school she wore a short gingham dress and American shoes and stockings. Now she was dressed like her mother, in an immensely full flounced skirt that swung around the ankles of her slim moccasins, and a basque waist of green velvet buttoned with much silver.

After the flock and Dezba had flowed sluggishly past the Family's fire and they had driven on again, they saw no more hogans and no more people. Three or four spirals of dust rising straight into the sunny sky like the smokes of campfires showed where other flocks must be grazing; and now and then a thin shimmer of real smoke indicated a hogan hidden behind a rise of ground; but that was the only further sign of human life. Soon, however, Father pointed with his whip at a sparkle of light above the horizon. It was the windmill that brought up the hidden water for their fields and for others near them. Before Vensi was completely starved they came in sight of the ranch-house, crouching low in the vast plain, its stone walls and adobe roof almost invisible in the sand — like a pebble dropped there, Vensi sometimes thought it looked.

She was weak from hunger when the mules at last clipped up to the dooryard, but other matters came before eating. Father unharnessed the team and led them to the cement trough at the windmill, Vensi following with the water-pails. At a turn of Father's wrist a shining stream rushed out of the spigot, a splendid thing to see. Vensi wished that she could lie under its cool freshness and soak it in through all her dry pores, drinking it at the same time. In this hot dry world, water was glorious.

The mules drank, and Father and Vensi drank, and Vensi
filled her pails. By this time a cow and two calves had
appeared, and then, with a great bleating, sheep poured
over a hillock and pelted toward the smell of water. Father
left it running slowly, since the shepherd would soon be
catching up with his flock and could be trusted to turn it
off.

Already Mother had spread her oilcloth on the ground
before the door, and had set out a kettle of stew and a
basket of piki. Soon the four were sitting in the delicious
shade, taking the edge from their hunger, while the hobbled
mules went rocking around the house, to get what good they
could of the sparse herbage.

In some ways the ranch-house was even happier than the
House on Top, for here the Family was alone in a blessed
solitude. The house was small, a single long room; but when
the sun blazed most fiercely, its thick stone walls, its thick
brush-and-adobe roof, kept it cool: Mother's windows, too,
were always made so that they could be opened; and the
sheltered entrance eastward offered shade and cool breezes.

There was plenty of work to do. First the beans must
be planted, and Father went at the task as soon as he had
done eating, Vensi helping him. This acre looked like clear
sand, so that a *bohanna* would not have guessed that it was
a field, except for its few posts and its strand of wire fencing.
The ceaseless wind had blown it into delicate ripples, dry
as powder.

A *bohanna* would not have guessed it was a field, but all
Hopis counted these patches of sand precious. Far and
wide on the desert every one was a field or an orchard — the
sunshiny flecks which could be seen from the House on Top
— for the deep layer of sand made a protecting blanket for
the life-giving moisture below. Wherever the sand slowly
drifted, there drifted the field. This one had spread
squarely across the road; but that was a defect easily

remedied: Father fenced in the patch and let the road bend around it.

He thrust through the sand with his planting-stick, and Vensi dropped beans into the hole and let it fill up again. She sang softly,

> 'One for the field mouse,
> One for the crow,
> One for the katchinas,
> And one to grow.'

Prairie dogs should have been mentioned, too, she thought, and bugs, and more than anything else the drought. Drought and wind together —— Grandmother's brother was the old man who each spring made an offering to the hot winds, on a sacred rock beside the mesa. It was an offering of cooked eggs, Vensi did not know why. Always 'Grandfather' made the offering; yet Vensi could not remember a time when the hot winds had not blown.

Throughout the afternoon the Family worked. Mother was busy in the house, making it livable again. With a twig broom she swept out the winter débris; in the box cupboards she stored the *tiposhoya's* supply of precious milk and Karo; and in a lard can, away from mice, the sack of wheat flour and the meal. Omva tagged her at every task, and the boy-baby now and then set up a small wail to say that he was hungry or wet, or that too many flies tickled his face and bare shoulders.

While the sunset worked its magic on mesas and buttes once more, and colored the billowing clouds, Father and Vensi finished their planting. Before they reached the house, their own flock came flooding over the rise toward the watering-trough, and Nuva followed them, dusty and sweaty with the day's long trek, the dog Askee nipping a few lagging heels.

Vensi stood by the corral gate and helped count the sheep and goats when they had drunk their fill and were

ready to pass into that irregular stockade of up-ended sap-
lings. Lambs and kids were squeaking with hunger. The
frail young ones that Father and Mother had carried in the
wagon were especially ravenous, but all were hungry, for
this evening Nuva had not let the flock tarry to feed.
Omva clung to Vensi's skirt and peered between her legs
in round-eyed interest as the little creatures demandingly
bunted their mothers; as the lambs plopped down on their
funny knees and lifted their heads to the feast; as the long-
eared kids, approaching the matter directly from the front,
swung their tails in rapid half-circles under the mother
goats' chins.

'Forty-five — forty-nine — fifty-one,' Nuva counted;
and Vensi nodded agreement.

'Run back to Mother,' Vensi bade Omva, shoving the
child gently in the direction of the house and then slipping
into the corral to help Nuva.

Some of the ewes and nanny-goats did not recognize the
babies that had been carried in the wagon, and some who
had twins refused to nurse them both. So Nuva bestrode a
reluctant mother, and Vensi tussled, laughing, with another, holding them until they became reconciled to the
woolly little heads that tugged at them.

Supper was awaiting the boy and girl on the floor of the
long, white-plastered room before they had managed to see
the babies all fed and had swung the crude corral gate back
into place and fastened it. The five — and the *tiposhoya* —
were together again.

A goat bleated, asking for something or other; a broken
sheep-bell clanked to itself; the crested flycatchers scolded
musically in the lone cottonwood tree; Askee barked with un-
warranted hopefulness after a prairie dog; a mule brayed.
Otherwise, complete stillness possessed the Family acres.
Yet even in the peace, with the flock safely corraled near by
and not another soul to be seen under the big bright sky, a
shadow disturbed the happiness.

'That Honawu,' Nuva mumbled, his voice thick with
fried bread, 'he asked have you made report of this new
tiposie to the Village Chief.'

Father's eyes sought the canopied cradle, from which
was coming a protesting mew. 'He is too small,' Father
joked. 'First we must be sure he is a real baby and not some
cricket or spider. Or perhaps a mosquito.'

Mother looked anxious. 'Maybeso we should have gone
to Uyi before we came here for the planting,' she said. 'You
know how it stands in the book the whites have printed for
us: that the Village Chief and the Council can choose the
guardians for the orphan child.'

'I do not see how Uyi can honestly object to us, and certainly no one else will be wanting the *tiposhoya*. Talk would
not plant the beans, and if they are so worried lest our
children should not be fattened, I think they will do well to
leave us alone at our planting,' Father said mildly.

'Uyi would not object to us if Honawu did not stir him
up,' Mother put in. 'But Honawu worries him like a dog
nipping at the horse's nose.'

'Why should that Honawu be so unfriendly?' Vensi
plumped out the query in the small voice that was yet
clear and round when she was with her own.

'I have heard him say,' Nuva offered, 'that he is no
friend to any Hopi who does not hold fast the Hopi ways.
And the Hopi gods.'

'I have done nothing more than go to their sewing-meet-
ings,' Mother said defensively. 'The *bohannas* from outside
send all those little pieces of cloth — I never could make
out why they go to all the trouble of cutting them up so
small, when we just sew them up again — and they send
them to us to make into quilts and ask not a thing in return.
Why waste all that? Besides, it is a pleasant thing to take
our dinner on those days and eat and talk together.'

'But they do sing songs and read from their Book about
the white god,' Father said gently.

'Then I turn my thoughts to other matters,' Mother retorted. 'Though from the little I have heard, there is nothing evil in their Way. It is cleaner than the Hopi Way,' she added in a husky voice, glancing round to make sure that no one was looking in at door or window. 'It is a Way that moves through the light.'

Vensi shivered at Mother's daring: Mother, custodian of the Old, Precious Things!

Father was gazing through an open window at the sky, darkening from flame to purple. 'The wise men have said,' he told them, 'that the time will come when the *bohanna* gods will sweep the Hopi gods from the face of the earth. Thus it has been written from the world's beginning. But they have also said that he is accursed who hastens that evil day, which we must hold off to the uttermost.'

'Mutz said,' Nuva continued hoarsely, 'that some of our people who should be strongest because they have influence — society heads and clan chiefs and Valuable Families — these are draining the tribe of strength by giving comfort and friendship to the *bohannas*.'

'Honawu and Mutz are witless to try to harass the *bohannas* as they do,' Father said calmly. 'As many as the sands of my fields, these whites. Drive one away and a hundred slide in and fill the hole he has left —— Three thousand and six hundred are the Hopis, I have heard; and I have also heard that for every single Hopi there are five hundred thousand *bohannas*. Five — hun-dred — thous-and,' Father repeated reflectively, leaning back to light a corn-husk cigarette from the stove: 'a number so great that it means nothing. But this I know: it would be as wise for a fly to fling itself into Oraibi Wash when it is running, to fight the drops of water there.'

Mother chuckled. 'Much talk you make; but the truth is that you like straight ways and kindness.'

Father smiled down at his glowing cigarette. 'Much talk

I make,' he agreed, 'but there is a clearer reason why
Honawu hates me. All day long he must listen to the wagging tongue of Lenmana, his wife, and all day long he hates
me because except for me he would never have taken in her
basket of piki and married her.'

Vensi and Nuva chuckled with him. This was not the
first time they had heard the story. Years ago, it seemed,
when these middle-aged parents were boy and girl, Honawu
had fancied Mother — Sivenka — and had hoped that she
would ask him to marry her. Not at all ugly was Sivenka
in those days, Father often said teasingly: much better-
looking, he usually added, than Vensi, who was so thin you
could not see her at all unless the sun was shining on her.
But Sivenka had not fancied the sharp-eyed Honawu, but
Father — Yoki — instead. And to Yoki's doorstep she had
carried her basket of piki, as was proper for a Hopi maid.

'You took it in fast enough,' Mother always reminded
him. Taking it in meant accepting the proposal.

'Yes,' Father would joke, 'I took it in because I thought
it was that rich girl, Tawamana, who had left the basket
there; and when I found out it was only poor little Sivenka
— well, I couldn't hurt her feelings by telling her my mis-
take.'

'If you had married Honawu,' Father reminded Mother
now, 'You would have brass beds and sugar and canned
peaches and tomatoes from the trader. If you had married
him, you and the children would be fat.'

'Mother's fried bread is as good as any tomatoes,' Vensi
said staunchly, looking down her nose at the thin crackly
brown crust before she set her teeth into it again.

'And we should be so fat that we need only roll downhill
instead of bothering to walk,' assented Mother, not men-
tioning the corpulent Lenmana by name. 'But I tell you
another thing: if I had married that one, in one week I think
he would have come home from the field and found sitting

out on the doorstep his saddle and the belt with the silver *conchos* as big as your hand.'

Father looked pleased. Putting out her husband's favorite possessions was a Hopi woman's way of divorcing him.

'A bad husband, maybeso,' Father agreed; 'and a bad enemy, surely.'

'Yet perhaps it is true that we should have no more to do with whites and with white ways,' Mother argued. 'These things that have happened to us, how can we be sure that Honawu or his followers have brought them to pass?'

'We cannot make others sure of it,' Father countered, 'for Honawu is as crooked and sly as a spider. But maybe some day the spider will catch himself in his own web, and then ——'

'Maybeso before that happens,' Nuva interrupted gloomily, 'he will have starved us to death and got Vensi, here, married to his sister's boy.'

Vensi shuddered. 'Wiki?' she whispered. 'Oh, I will not!'

Mother looked at her compassionately. 'No, certainly not,' she said. 'And if we are to be such right Hopis, we will not let our thoughts travel these dark paths. Come, we must clear away the food and to bed.'

Washing the dishes was a small matter: the bowl that had held the stew and the frying-pan that had held the bread. Going to bed was a small matter: each spreading his sheepskin on the floor, which had only just got through being the table, slipping off shoes and outer garments, lying down and covering himself with a quilt against the quick coolness of the desert night.

Through the south window Vensi could see the Star Dipper, and through the door the Crowd of Stars. For at least five minutes she lay awake, watching the Crowd begin to climb the sky. Her thoughts were unhappily busy with the lumbering, clumsy Wiki.

When Wiki was a little boy, she recalled, he used to string
live bumblebees with a needle and thread. Nowadays, she
felt sure, he relished clipping the burros' ears when they
broke into his parents' cornfields. Certainly the Hopi law
allowed you to clip a burro's ears when he stole from you,
Vensi sleepily admitted to herself; but you needn't enjoy
doing it.

There was the matter of Askee, too. The kind old grizzled
mongrel was unlike the numberless curs that snarled and
skulked and starved around the villages. He even had a
name, which most of them had not. 'Askee' was Navajo
for 'Boy,' and Father had named him thus because the dog
reminded him of a laughing Navajo lad who had been his
friend. Askee himself laughed, jaws wide, tongue lolling.

Wiki, however, he did not like; and when he ran out to
bark at the boy, Wiki had been so frightened that he had
stepped into a crevice and bruised his right ankle. Thereupon he had hurled a jagged stone at the dog's right ankle,
almost breaking it. Only lately had Askee ceased limping;
and with all his heart he hated Wiki, greeting his approach
with a crescendo of growls and barks quite unlike his usual
mild objections. Yes, Wiki had a perfect right to hurt the
dog's ankle, when the dog had made him hurt his; but, right
or not, Vensi disliked him for the deed.

All night she dreamed of burros and Askee and Wiki,
and it was a relief to be wakened. Mother wakened her,
stepping over her to make a fire to warm the milk for the
boy-baby. Already the sun was a keen red blade cutting
the edge of the earth, and the sheep were bleating in the
corral, and the birds were quarreling in the cottonwood, and
there was no Wiki anywhere near; and the morning was
good.

Both good and bad was the day that grew out of it. Nuva,
going to drive the sheep to graze, came running back, his
face long. 'Coyotes!' he grunted. 'They have squeezed
through into the corral and stolen two lambs.'

Father aimed a kick at Askee. It was a disgusted kick, but not one that would hurt: the dog merely removed himself a foot or two, tail drooping.

'Why didn't you make more fuss about it?' Father scolded him. 'Only through my dreams did I hear you growl. . . . Tonight we chain you at the corral gate.'

'*Okiway*,' Mother mourned, albeit philosophically. 'Two lambs, which would have been two muttons. More hungry days.'

'Less hope for a dress from the mail-order catalogue,' thought Vensi. 'Less hope for shiny shoes.'

Otherwise, though, the day was good. First, there was the boy-baby. There was no change in him that Vensi could see with her eyes or feel with her fingers; but Mother said he was stronger; and he was stronger. Sometimes, too, he slept from feeding to feeding.

He continued to fascinate Omva dangerously, but Father partly solved that problem. He fetched in from the corral one of the prettiest and smallest of the kids, and it diverted the big baby's attention from the little baby. The kid was an engaging creature, with tight brown-and-white curls and spaniel-like ears and an expression of noble dignity and patience. It was so small that Omva could lug it around, her shoulders hunched high to keep its feet from dragging; and she could even catch it again when it managed to make its escape.

On this good day there was a good change in diet, too. While Nuva herded his sheep he gathered a kettleful of salt-weed greens, young and tender, and the pods left by the waxy yucca blossoms, still soft so that they were good when baked for the noon meal.

Even the change of work was pleasant. There was plenty to fill the whole day, but it was different from the tasks on Top. For one thing, the early corn was up, and it kept everyone busy, for the waves of sand were already flowing

over it. They would flow over it faster than it could grow
above them, unless each stalk was scooped free and protected by a small shelter of brush.

When the shelters were attended to, the corn must be
watered, to discourage the insects that were attacking it.
Vensi helped Father with the watering. The two took
water-pails and handleless brooms and walked between the
rows dipping the brooms in water, and sprinkling the plants
one by one. Father's face was ruddy through its brown before they had done. The bright sand and the green rows
shimmered before Vensi's hot eyes, and sweat-bees clung to
her damp clothing and stung.

Father said thoughtfully, 'In my father's day we had no
water for our fields except what little we could carry from
the springs; and the springs were small and feeble and often
choked with sand.'

Vensi murmured in her throat, wanting him to go on.

'The *bohanna* is in some ways evil, I grant you; but it is
the *bohanna*, our Water-Witch among them, who knows
where to pierce the earth and bring up the underground
rivers; and it is the Water-Witch who has cleansed and
guarded many of our ancient springs that had strangled to
uselessness. Not for his own use. No. For the Hopi and of
course also for the Navajo . . . Whatever Honawu says ——
But I do not see,' he broke off uneasily, 'why the men do
not come to help with the shearing.'

Was it only by chance, Vensi wondered, that Father's
words ran from Honawu to the neighbors who had as yet
failed to come to the aid of the Family? Or did Father
think that Honawu had a hand in the matter? She con-
cluded that it was only by chance: Father's quick ears had
perhaps heard the approach of the unseen flock; had heard
the broken sheep-bell. Now the sheep appeared out of the
sky at the crest of a dune, and came pouring downward, a
gray-white river.

It had always given Vensi happiness to see a flock of sheep, dull white sharpened with black, flowing homeward over a big lonely earth. She had never pinned the happiness down, never understood its cause, until Nuva explained it to her.

It made a picture, he said, and pictures naturally gave happiness. He tried to copy this one on a piece of wrapping paper, with wax crayons that Miss McClung had given him. There had been no crayon at all for the deep and tender blue of the sky; and he found his hands too clumsy to get the look of the sheep, rounded and soft and solid. For an hour he worked, sweating, and then he crumpled the paper and burned it, and went away where nobody could find him.

Tonight also he was somber. 'The men do not come to shear?' he asked anxiously. 'These sheep are too hot. This afternoon I could find little shade for them, and they kept crowding together to make their own shade. I was afraid they might even smother themselves, as in the snow.'

'We may have to shear by ourselves,' said Father.

Next morning they began. Mother was a good hand with the shears and Nuva was not bad. Most of the time Vensi was kept busy looking after Omva and the boy-baby and boiling the coffee and making the dinner; but when there was a chance she, too, sheared a sheep, Father throwing the heavy beast and tying it for her.

'*Lolama*, good!' Mother commended when Vensi laid back one side of the bulky, smelly fleece almost as one would lay back a coat, without leaving a smudge of red on the sheared skin. And '*Okiway*, too bad!' she softly lamented when the heavy 'chewing-iron' slipped in Vensi's slim hand and scored that sheared flesh with red. Vensi hated to hurt the poor creature, it was so helpless and still. Sometimes she thought the *bohannas* were right, and animals felt pain as people felt.

Even with all the Family working, they hadn't got far with the flock when at noon they sat down in the porch shade to eat.

'A wagon comes,' Nuva announced suddenly, jerking his head toward Second Mesa. There was not enough dust for a flock, but there was dust.

'The shearers, maybeso,' Mother said hopefully. 'If that is so, daughter, we shall have time to gather yucca for the flat baskets, this afternoon, and dyestuffs for the fancy baskets.' Mother was a famous weaver, but she and Vensi had hard work finding time to gather all her materials.

They all sat with eyes fixed on the dust column, but when the wagon came in sight Father shook his head. 'I don't think,' he said. 'The horses are not from our mesa.'

'Oraibi,' said Mother.

Oraibi they were, people from the farthest of the three Hopi mesas. Toward the ranch-house they swerved, and the driver, standing in his wagon, stopped his team and called out in the lilting tone of the Oraibi, who leaves the ends of his sentences hanging in the air.

'Where are you going?' Father asked politely, going out to stand with a foot on the wheel-hub.

'We go to Painted Desert,' the Oraibi man answered. 'We have come by way of Middle Village, and there Pone-oma asked me to say to you that he has an illness and cannot help with your shearing. Also Lomavitu is prevented. By sore nose in his own flock, he says, so that he must care for his beasts with the brown stuff the Agent told us of.'

'*Okiway!*' Mother moaned on a sucked-in breath. 'Now we must finish alone.'

Vensi felt all at once stiffer and sorer and more sunburnt. So much remained to be done.

The Oraibi went on. 'One has told me,' he said, his eyes flickering past the group, 'that the new *Mongwi*, Agent, wishes you to come at once to the Canyon. You and your family. It is something about an orphan baby. I think perhaps the Village Council complained.'

Father expelled a sharp breath. 'Go to the Canyon, when sheep are to shear and fields to tend, and when the hot sun and wind are busy burning and burying the corn? The Council must have been in great haste. Who has told you this, my friend?'

'Who? I do not remember. But he said, "Now; today; or perhaps for you and yours bad trouble."' And, bracing himself on his calico-clad legs, he slapped the reins over his horses' bony backs and drove away, leaving the Family to stare at each other in blank dismay.

'WHAT is to be done is to be done,' said Father. 'Words won't change the matter.'

At once the Family made ready to go to the Canyon. Vensi scurried to pack the necessary clothes and food and bedding into the wagon, while Mother attended to the boy-baby.

Without moving him overmuch, she oiled him carefully; for at the hospital she had learned to oil Omva. She mixed milk and water and Karo ready to be heated for his next feeding. He was asleep when she set his small tent into the wagon-bed, on a pile of sheepskins which would cushion the bumps.

The Family would certainly be gone today and next day, and Nuva must stay with the sheep. He had never before had the entire responsibility for so long a time, but he was sixteen, or maybe seventeen, and must accept burdens.

Last summer he had been initiated into the clan, staying
down in the kiva for a month and eating no salt in his food
during those weeks. Legally, he was a man.

Yet as the rest of the Family drove away from the ranch-
house and the grazing flock, the new man looked like a
lonesome boy. He stood there with his denim legs sturdily
apart and his short schoolboy hair tied back from his face
with a rag of yellow silk. As was his way, he scowled and
grinned at the same time, his eyebrows down over his eyes
and his teeth flashing white. Vensi thought that even when
he was cross he was better than any other boy on the mesa
— better than any other boy on the three mesas.

Askee lay at his feet, nose on paws and eyes watchful,
wanting to go with the horses and knowing that he must
stay with the sheep. Looking at him, Father remembered.

'Be sure to tie Askee to the corral gate. And you had
best sprinkle the corn tonight when the sun touches Second
Mesa.'

Vensi said: 'The kid Omva has been playing with,
Brother, have you seen it about? And when you find it,
will you take it to its mother?'

And Mother said: 'Mutton bones are in the pot, and
there are bread and piki enough. Cook yourself coffee and
beans, my son.' She clucked in her throat as she watched
him from the tail of the wagon, standing so straight and
still.

It was a warm day, and Mother hastened to roll up the
wagon-cover so that the air could flow through and make
a coolness as they rode. 'Okiway!' she cried, when she
had nudged Omva aside so that she could manage the
canvas. 'Now, how could so small a one get it up there?'

Father screwed around in his seat to look, and Vensi
wriggled back in the wagon-bed. There against the side,
with Omva's arms tight round his neck, lay the pet kid.

Father softly hissed his vexation, while Omva kept a

watchful silence. 'There is no time to take it back,' said Father, 'but what will it do for food?'

Omva's expression lost its wariness, and she tightened her arms in a relieved hug of the curly neck. The kid's eyes bulged and it gave a strangled squeak.

'Oh, naughty baby!' Vensi reproached. 'Now you are choking the life out of him.'

Father loosened his head kerchief with one hand and tossed it back. 'This banda,' he said, 'it is almost split in two. Take one of the strips and make a collar. Then Omva will have something to get hold of.'

Vensi divided the ragged red banda and tied it in a firm bowknot around the small neck, and Omva, with a chortle of delight, dragged the decorated baby farther up in her lap. Vensi turned her attention once more to the road and the wayside.

At first the sky had been a bowl turned over them, pale blue in the hot brightness, like poor turquoise. A cornfield they passed showed the blades ruffled and drooping, and the plains were hard and blank. But now, as the mules labored through the deep sand of the road, the sun was veiled by filmy cloud and the plain dappled to softness by its shadow.

'Rain, do you think?' Vensi wondered. 'So early in the summer?'

'Good if it were,' said Father. 'Our beans would jump out of the ground. But there is no wetness in those clouds. Only wind. Only sand.'

Already the wind was rising in the east, moaning under the wagon-top so that Vensi and Mother let the sides down again. Gradually the pale turquoise of the sky canopied itself with copper. And not alone the sky was changing, but the road. It crept toward the eastward-moving wagon, so that even the brisk mules seemed marking time against its current. The road crept toward them, and in sandy

stretches the land on either side flowed with it. Nothing
was still.

'The *tiposhoya*,' Vensi asked fearfully, 'maybeso the
wind will steal his breath away.'

Mother put another quilt over his cradle-bow, clucking
anxiously.

That wind seemed bound to snatch even the breath of
the older and stronger. Omva bowed over the little goat
and buried her face in her sister's lap. Now and then she
peered out from her refuge, blinking her eyes and gasping
with half-pleasurable fear. The sand was driven under
eyelids, between lips; teeth gritted on it and skin grew
sore under its pelting.

The mules needed urging now: they wanted to turn tail
to the storm as was their nature. Father struck them
lightly with the rope end of his whip, watching through
the slits of his lids for the spring and the cottonwoods he
had hoped to reach.

'*Antsa*, truly, we should have reached them before this,'
he muttered. 'Daughter, can your young eyes see any
shadow of them?'

Vainly Vensi peered through the thickening copper.
The keenest vision could pierce only a few feet of it. The
wagon was swathed with a million veils, overhead, before,
behind, to the right hand, to the left.

Once something shadowed the curtains into which the
mules thrust their unwilling muzzles, and, coming through
layer after layer, vaguer and larger than life, grew more
distinct until it became a burro with a small Navajo boy
crouched on its back and a full-skirted Navajo woman
leading it. With only a sidewise and upward glance from
her bowed head she passed them and was shut away by
the curtains behind.

Soon after that, Father tightened his reins and brought
the team to a stop. 'I am off the road, I think,' he told

Vensi, who rose on her knees and peered out over the wagon-seat.

Working blindly, he unharnessed the mules and tied them to a wheel, so that they could turn their rumps into the storm and droop their heads in the slight shelter of the wagon. Then he clambered down into the wagon-bed and huddled himself under quilts with the rest of the Family. So they sat for an hour, with no sounds but wind and sand sounds, except when the mules brayed.

'Someone passing on the road, maybeso,' Father commented then, his voice muffled by the quilts.

Vensi, peering out, could not yet see anyone passing, nor any road for him to pass on.

At last, little by little, the wind died away and the sand settled, and the Family shook itself free of its gritty coverings and climbed out to see where it was.

'Look!' Vensi called, pointing with her chin and laughing. Not a hundred feet away rose the dusty cottonwoods and the oblong cement trough which 'Washindon' — and the Water-Witch — had built above the spring. So near had they been to their goal and yet unknowing.

Father grunted his amused disgust and hitched up the mules again and drove in under the shelter of the trees. There he built a small fire, and the womenfolks fed the baby and made the evening meal. It was still and peaceful after the storm, and, though there was grit in everything, it was good to have shelter and breath and food.

Nor did the sand make bad beds, when places had been scooped out to fit bodies. Vensi woke once or twice, but only to turn over and listen a minute to the yapping of coyotes or the hoot of an owl, or to blink through sleep-sticky eyes at the stars, so big and bright and near. When the *tiposhoya* was still, Father and Mother were snoring in a reassuring way, and Vensi drifted back into sleep again without knowing it.

Then it was morning, and the flycatchers were chattering noisily in the cottonwood branches, and Yapa, the mockingbird, was singing and scolding and talking all at the same time. Mother had already heated milk and was holding the basket-cradle on her lap and reaching under its protecting canopy to feed the tiny boy.

'The wind did not harm him, nor yet the sand,' she told Vensi with soft triumph, and turned back the cover so that she could see. 'Look for yourself: he is not only no worse; he is better. Isn't the pink in his skin more? And the blue shadows under his eyes, are they not less?'

Vensi scrutinized the small old face seriously. 'Yes,' she answered with glad conviction, 'pinker he is, and not so blue; not so much as if you could see through him.'

While Mother finished feeding him, Vensi made dough for the bread. Wheat flour and salt, baking-powder and water, they had brought with them. It was no trick at all to add water and make the dough. As she had often watched Mother do, Vensi patted bits of the dough into balls that grew flatter and flatter as she tossed them between her well-scrubbed palms.

'You are not so bad at it,' Mother approved, watching her over the cradle.

'It is so easy when you do it, but so hard when I do,' said Vensi — 'to get just enough hold in the middle without having it look like a worn-out saddle blanket.'

She laid a grate across two stones above the smoldering greasewood fire, raked back the embers a little, and slapped the saucer-sized biscuits down on the cross-bars. They were as good as fried bread, if eaten while still fresh; and the Family seldom left a crumb to grow cold and tough.

'Omva, wake up!' Mother called. 'Breakfast is almost ready. Stir yourself, little sleepyhead.'

The humped-up blanket under the wagon did not move. Laughing, Vensi dived at it, ready to lift out the warm, sleepy sweetness. Omva was so cuddly when she woke: not cross, but clinging and dear.

Vensi's hands plunged into empty folds of blanket. 'Mother!' she gasped. 'She is not here.'

'Hiding in the wagon?' Mother suggested briskly.

She was not hiding in the wagon.

'What is all this running to and fro?' Father called through his wet hands from the watering-trough, where he had been washing himself. 'You hunt the kid, maybeso?'

'Not the kid,' Vensi quavered: 'Omva.'

Father's face came out of his hands, startled and protesting.

'That could not be, a small weak thing like Omva,' he said, but his eyes jumped back to the trough and ran its length, before the sudden tension of his face loosened. 'Let us look quickly,' he said, 'everywhere there is a place to hide. And call.'

They called: 'Omva! Omva! Come, Little Sister!' as they scurried around the camp place. It took very few minutes to make sure that there was no Omva huddled on the far side of tank or trough, trees or wagon.

'In the books,' said Vensi, remembering stories her teachers had read aloud, 'Indians could track a baby as easily as following a beetle-trail in the sand.'

'Books!' Father said scornfully. 'Books by whites. And look: yesterday blew the sand into a fine cover, but every hour the breeze is busy sweeping it clear of trails.'

'If she had had a bright dress, even,' murmured Mother, over a catch in her throat. 'Once it was yellow, but it has faded and faded ——'

There were few places to hide, and many. Every clump of saltweed, of sagebrush, of greasewood, of rabbit-brush, could hide a mischievous squatting baby in a faded yellow dress. And those clumps, all rounded to globes by the steady wind, were like the stars of the sky for number. It made Vensi's stomach churn to think how many there were, and how many sheltered a coiled and rattling death.

'Vensi, daughter,' said Father, 'if you ride one mule and I the other, we can make widening circles, searching ——'

He leaped to the back of one, and Vensi grabbed the roached mane of the other, pulled herself up on her stomach, flung a leg across. They rode, each making half the circle and widening it when they met.

It would be so easy, Vensi thought sickly, for the little figure to slip past, to slip past in a hollow, without seeing them or being seen by them. And the little hollows, like the globed plants, were without number. If Omva had only a few more years she would recognize Flat-Topped Butte; she would know the outline of First Mesa, of Second Mesa, there on the sky, plain as a small word in a reading-book, and she could steer toward one or the other. But now ——

For an hour they rode, their eyes aching with the steadiness of their search. 'It is impossible that she should go so far, even if she wandered away when we first roused,' Father said flatly, meeting Vensi. 'We must close in again.'

They sat looking back toward the cottonwoods and their wagon. Suddenly Father roofed his eyes with his palm against the still level sun.

'Your mother!' he ejaculated. 'She waves a rag.'

He clapped his heels into the mule's sides and was off, Vensi following. As they drew nearer, they could see that Mother, clinging to the wagon-bows, was pointing, and they turned their mounts in the direction she indicated.

'Look!' called Vensi, thrusting out an eager chin.

On a little hillock against the sky something lifted like a dry leaf, settled, lifted, the sun burning through it as through a scarlet cactus flower.

'There is red!' said Vensi. 'It is the piece of your banda. It is the pet kid.'

'The kid' — the words were jolted out of Father as he rode. 'It was gone, then, too.'

Not until they were within a few rods of the bouncing little goat could they make out the faded yellow of Omva's dress, almost invisible in the desert. She had pulled off one moccasin, and sat hugging her foot and crying softly.

'Pins!' she explained, when they came up to her. 'Pins in feet!'

Laughing and scolding, Father swung her up across his mule's neck, and in a few minutes they were back at the campsite. An acrid smell of burned bread hovered on the air, and Vensi's loaves lay like broken charcoal disks, at one side of the fire. But Mother already had more loaves baking on the grill.

There had never been better bread, and even though there was not enough, no one minded. Vensi shivered with relief and delight when Omva climbed on her back and laid her little head in the nape of Vensi's neck. And Father gave the bleating kid a little milk, letting it suck his fingers. For who knew what might have happened if that kid had not been along? Maybe, without him, Omva would not have lost herself. But maybe, once lost, she would not have been found. Not soon enough.

'*Okiway* ——' Mother said suddenly, as if she were thinking of some dreadful possibility.

And that was all the Family said about the losing and the finding.

Just before noon the mules clicked across the cattle-guard grating and between the gateposts of the Agency. It was exciting to visit the Agency. Government school and hospital and office, homes of Government workers, two churches and a mission house, all were dropped into the winding canyon against a sheer cliff wall. At one end was a marvelous water tank set high in the rocks: a barrel, Vensi thought, bigger than a house, and giving water, without toil, to all these hundreds of people.

There were grassy lawns to admire — the only lawns Vensi had ever seen — and the dusty green feathers of the tamarisk, abloom with dusty pink feathers. And there was the school building itself, gutted by fire since last the

Family had visited the Canyon. The moving-picture apparatus had set fire to the schoolhouse. Vensi sighed with regret. Once, when they had come to the Canyon, the whole electric system had been off, as it often was; and another time the moving-picture machine had been out of repair. She had hoped that the next time there would be a picture show and she could at last witness the wonder of pictures that moved and spoke.

However, today would hold excitement: something special was happening, for more than the usual number of inhabitants were visible: the school athletic field was black with people.

Father chirped to his team. 'A gathering of the folks,' he said, 'to know the new Mongwi, Chief, maybeso.'

The roads were lined with wagons and saddle-ponies. Navajo heads in broad-brimmed, high-crowned Stetsons rose above those of the shorter Hopis. Comfortably plump Hopi women drew a little apart from the lean, hawk-faced Navajo ones. All turned toward the small, round-faced man in spectacles who stood on a box and spoke to them.

Father drove as close as he could and stopped his team and they listened.

'Mutz, he interprets for the new Mongwi,' Vensi murmured distastefully. 'Where, do you think, is the regular interpreter?'

Mutz often interpreted. He had spent long years in school and his English was good.

'The people laugh to themselves at the words of Mongwi,' said Mother, listening attentively to Mutz's translation. 'They seem foolish words, but of course he is a *bohanna*.'

'It is not the words of Mongwi that are foolish; it is the words of Mutz,' Father amended.

Vensi kneeled up against the side of the wagon to listen and watch, and Omva clung to her shoulders so that she could see these alarming throngs and yet hide quickly if they made a move toward her. The Indians were standing straight and quiet, their faces masklike. Only by the smallest murmurous asides; only by the quality of their silence and lack of expression, did the Family know that they were laughing. Mongwi did not guess it; he went right on, his face growing pink with earnestness, his round glasses catching the sun.

Vensi studied him curiously, for on him might depend her happiness. Every time a new Mongwi came to the Agency, the council of Middle Village presented to him their complaints, and often these complaints included Father. This Mongwi was trim and spotless, in khaki and shiny leather puttees, and his hands and feet were as small and neat as an Indian's. His hair was thick and fair, like the boy-baby's, and his nose was surprisingly long. A Navajo near them muttered something, and Father's smile-lines deepened.

'The Navajo says this chief must be named Chief Baby-Owl — Chief Owlet,' Father said.

'I am a small man,' Mongwi was saying, shouting to make them hear, 'but behind me stands the Great White Father, larger than these hills. The Great White Father has much to give you, and his wish is to help you ——'

Mutz took up the words smoothly, in the Hopi and then in the Navajo. He was clever about it, Mutz: he even waved his hands as Mongwi did, pounding one neat fist into the other palm, with just an added flourish that burlesqued the gesture; and his interpretation was so like Mongwi's words that those Indians who knew little English might think he was translating fairly. Vensi was at first only puzzled; but Mother took it all as a fair translation; Mother knew many English words, but she got lost as soon as a *bohanna* worked up steam.

'I am a great white father,' Mutz piped. 'I am larger than these hills. The Great White Father has much to

give his red children; or if he will he can take much from
them ——'

'A crooked tongue,' Father muttered, his kind face setting into its stern lines and his eyes flashing. 'Take the
reins for me, daughter.'

Vensi climbed up and gathered the reins into her trembling hand. Father would take action: you could see that.
Crookedness he could not endure. And if he took action,
here in the public eye, Mutz would be angrier than ever;
and then Honawu would be angrier, too. And, besides,
everyone would stare at the Family. With one hand Vensi
pulled her shawl close around her face, against that proba-
bility. Behind her, Mother clucked questioningly.

'My friend shares a joke with you,' Father said clearly
to the people in the Hopi tongue, 'or else he did not catch
all of Mongwi's words. Mongwi has said that he is a small
man, but that the Father behind him is large and strong
and wills good to his children the People, the Hopis, and
Those-With-Good-Foreheads, the Navajos.'

The listeners shifted their feet and some of them now
really laughed. Mutz laughed, too, as if he had indeed
joked; but his eyes sprang blackly at Father. And the new
Agent, thinking Father the cause of the laughter, frowned
at him with the quick anger of a small man's hurt dignity,
and waved him aside.

Mother, not yet fully understanding, murmured on a
sucked-in-breath, '*Okiway*, now why is Mongwi angry
with your father?'

Vensi's dismayed heart flopped like a pollywog within
her ribs.

When this introductory talk was over, the Family sought
the office building and stood silent before the Agent's desk,
waiting his pleasure. The Agent recognized Father and
frowned.

'Well, and what is it now?' he asked stiffly.

'You send for us. We come,' Father answered with dignity. 'The beans been to planting, and the sheep to shearing. And we a whole day by wagon.'

'Well?' the Agent asked, his nose pompous.

'The baby, she got only a few days yet: six, maybeso.'

'You let the mother lug that great heavy cradle when the child is less than a week old?' the Agent demanded.

Father stared at him, thoroughly confused. 'You send for us. We come,' he repeated.

'I didn't send for you,' the Agent contradicted. 'It seems to me there's a lot of funny business around here, my good fellow ... But how can she get enough air, with all those heavy quilts over her?'

He was up and around the desk quickly, and plucking gingerly at the covers. Mother braced the cradle against her knee and laid them back.

'But this can't be your child!' the Agent exclaimed, staring at the small oat-colored head.

'No,' Father agreed, 'she a throwed-away boy-baby.'

The Agent whistled. 'She — he — looks as if it would be better off in the hospital,' he said.

Mother did not understand the words, but the Agent's tone and gesture were clear enough so that she swept a protective arm across the cradle and backed away.

Father fumbled for English words and gave up. 'You explain to Mongwi how small the boy-baby was; how thin,' he bade Vensi.

The hot blood rushed to Vensi's face and heart till she was almost suffocated. Nuva often talked for Father, having his school English, stumbling enough, but far better than Father's; but Vensi —— She shrank into herself and her eyes grew big with fright.

'The baby, it was not took no care of,' she whispered, sliding her eyes back to Father for support. 'One whole day, they say, no milk, no water, no bathings ... The

Mission-Mary, she find it outside his door. But she can't —
she can't eat it. So he send for my mother — Sivenka.'
Vensi jerked her head, birdlike, toward her mother, and
took time off to moisten her lips and haul her breath down
where it belonged. 'My mother make us strong when we
small and weak; she know very good how to do babies.
This one, now it eating and sleeping and getting fat.'

She retired, sweating, behind Mother, and Omva, who
had hold of her skirts, retired behind her.

'Fat!' snorted the Agent, scowling at the baby as if
the sight hurt him.

Miss Rivers, a red-haired woman who was one of the
Government workers, passed through the hall and paused
to see who the group of Hopis might be. She smiled at
them and came in and spoke under her breath to the
Agent, looking at the Family sidewise as she talked.

Vensi tried to hear what Miss Rivers said without ap-
pearing to listen, but the white woman spoke low and fast
and her words were hard to understand:

'They do that, the Hopis: disown the child if its mother
dies. It's almost unheard of for a Hopi to adopt such an
infant, but this family — why, this would make four ...'
Her voice slurred so that Vensi could make out only the
final words: ' ... some complaint by their fellow-villagers.'

'Complaint?'

'That they can't take proper care of the children, for
one thing. They're poverty poor. Bad luck seems to
follow the man ——'

'There's usually a reason for bad luck and the dislike of
neighbors,' the Agent suggested curtly.

Vensi stood drooping there, pretending to look at the
baskets and pottery and big colored ears of corn in the
glass wall-cases. The Agent's words gave her more fear to
eat, and it lay like a stone in her stomach.

'I suppose usually,' the red-haired Miss Rivers answered

slowly, 'but in this case it doesn't seem quite so clear. Sometimes jealousy and an old feud ... There's a group that's forever complaining about this couple for one thing or another, but personally I like them better than I do the ones that make the complaints.'

The Agent turned back to Father. 'Don't you really believe,' he asked more kindly, 'that you and your good wife had better leave the two babies at the hospital here, where they'd get the best of care and grow fat?'

Omva was peeking around Vensi's skirt at the Agent now, and he stretched out a quick hand and pinched her brown cheek gently. The baby girl melted out of sight.

'It might even be wise to put this older one where she could have better food,' he added, his eyes passing from Vensi's thin face down her patched dress to her ragged shoes. 'It might be better for you all.'

Mother looked anxiously from one to the other and edged toward the door. Father looked straight ahead, eyes blank. Vensi gave a despairing little mouse-squeak. For this was too terrible. First the desert had tried to steal away Omva, this precious weight that hung to her knees, and now, before the day was far gone, the Agent; and not only Omva did he try to take, but the *tiposhoya* and Vensi herself.

'No, no, please!' she whispered. 'Fatness is not everything. Me, I too, too strong.'

'Strong! A stiff breeze would carry you off,' the Agent declared. 'And can't you talk out loud? ... Well, we'll wait awhile and see what we shall see. Give these children plenty of milk, my good woman, and fruit and vegetables. And eggs. Then we'll see —— By the way, what is the blond young man's English name? Or is it a blonde young woman, instead? Half the time you've called it him and half the time her.'

'The Hopi pronouns haven't any gender,' Miss Rivers

explained, with a reassuring smile at Vensi. 'It makes our
hims and *hers* very confusing to learn. Boy?' she asked
Father.

Mongwi had been gesturing toward the cradle, so that
Father had followed his queer talk.

'Boy,' he said. 'You picked her name?' he asked Vensi.

Vensi had given much thought to the matter, and had
talked it over with Mother, also. From field matrons and
teachers and Mission-Marys, even from chance visitors,
came many of the English names on the mesas. She herself
had been named Fern by a field matron, and she had always
hated it. It had no meaning for her, though the teacher
said that there were plants called Fern in other parts of
the world. She had taken pains to choose an understand-
able name for Omva: Shirley Temple. On the big pencil
tablets at the trading-post there were colored paper-dolls
named Shirley Temple and Jane Withers and Sandra.
Vensi had thought of calling the boy-baby Sandra, but
she had decided to name him instead for her favorite picture
at school, one with a flag draped over it.

She stood on tiptoe and whispered into Father's bent-over
ear.

Father took a minute to arrange the syllables in his
mouth.

'Aberaham Linkum,' he announced.

THE Family started for the ranch at once, so that they might reach it before nightfall. This time they would drive to First Mesa and take the desert road from that point.

First Mesa was a rock ship sailing the gray-brown billows of the desert. The cut-out-paper shapes at its top were the outlines of its three villages. Near its base clustered school buildings and another group of mission buildings and the Water-Witch's little Mexican-style house, and Lomavoya's trading-post. Today there was something more: on the slope behind the trading-post sat a house trailer. The Family had seen house trailers before, but never one like this. Who could have imagined a silver house, and in shape like a flattened egg?

'I have heard of this house-on-wheels,' said Father,

stopping before the store. 'The man who runs it around the
world is evil, they say. He comes to get treasures from the
People.'

'To steal?' Vensi inquired.

'He gives money for what the people bring to him,'
Father admitted. 'But it is said that he also breaks into
the graves. Is it anything but evil to take from the dead
what their families have buried with them?' he demanded
indignantly. 'That is the reason the Village Chiefs will not
let him camp nearer the villages.'

Still peering at the silver house, the Family climbed
the steps to the trading-post. It was always an alluring
place to visit: there was so much to eat in it. The shelves
were solidly lined with cans and boxes; and in the back
towered the white-and-silver wonder of the electric re-
frigerator, from which, when the electricity was running,
bottles of pop came frosty-cold as winter, even in the
hottest summertime.

Father and Nuva always had an eye for the high-crowned
Stetson hats and the cowboy boots, and Mother and Vensi
for the gay handkerchiefs and blankets and the bolts of
cloth. In the balcony were piles of Navajo blankets, head-
high, and baskets from Second Mesa and Oraibi; and in a
long side room the pottery of First Mesa, as many bowls
and jars as could be used in ten years. The trading-post
was a cave of wonders, though its much food sometimes
made Vensi dizzy with longing.

Today it was less beautiful by reason of a tall white
man, who lounged against a counter amid Hopis and
Navajos. Also, one of the Hopis was Mutz, who must have
driven out of the Canyon as soon as the speech was done.

'This *bohanna* is the grave-robber of whom I told you,'
Father said under his breath. 'We will listen and learn
what he has to say.'

Mother let the cradle down on a counter and they all

stood at ease. They had come in to buy a box of matches only; but even if the *bohanna* had not been there to provide free entertainment, they would have got their money's worth. They would have studied the peaches and strawberries, the solid red tomatoes, the huge green peas that decorated the can labels; they would have decided within themselves which boots and which shawls they would have bought if they had had any money; and perhaps the safe door would have been open and they would have tried to identify the pawned jewelry that hung there in such opulence of silver and shell and turquoise.

Now, with this *bohanna* looking on, Vensi could not slide silently along the counter as usual, filling her eyes. Besides, he was saying something that interested her. She stood with her eyes fixed on the floor and her attention on the speaker.

'So you worship the albinos as children of the sun?' the archaeologist asked Mutz, glancing at a small albino Navajo girl as he spoke. Her hair was bound into a startlingly lovely golden butterfly that perched above the black velvet collar of her blouse. 'That's something I never heard mentioned before.'

'Yes, that is true,' Mutz answered, his eyes wide with candor and his round face bland. Vensi thought resentfully, *He looks like a good child, with his shining black bob of hair neatly twisted about with green silk; and his fat hands are stiff with silver and turquoise while Father's must go bare.*

He went on: 'And the Sun Clan *tiponi* — like one of these here king's spectres it is — it's got the clippings of their hair in the middle of its ear of corn. Yes, it sure does. They can't ever throw away the smallest clipping ——'

Mutz's yarn went on and on. The lounging Indians were still, and Lomavoya himself leaned up against the wall with his good-humored face expressionless. Vensi sucked in her cheeks to keep from laughing, and Father

listened enjoyably, as to any other tall tale. No need for
him to straighten out this crookedness: the *bohanna* de-
served what he was getting. To rob the living was not good,
but how much worse to rob the dead! And to rob them of
possessions which their families had sacrificed for the
enrichment of their departed spirits!

'There is another secret I would tell few *bohannas*,'
Mutz went on, 'and it has to do with the dances-for-rain.'

'But what about all these people here?' the archaeologist
asked curiously. 'Won't they object to your telling secret
things?'

'Oh, these!' Mutz dismissed them lightly. 'They do
not know enough English to understand. Except my good
friend the trader, and he is your friend, too, and the friend
of this National Museum of yours. So he will not mind.'

Lomavoya only smiled, the rather embarrassed yet
fatherly smile he kept for *bohannas*.

'It is this way,' said Mutz: 'If the Snake Dance does
not bring the rains in August, the clan fathers choose the
youngest and most beautiful of these albinos, and take
them up to the notch in the mesa where the sun sits down
in the wettest time of year. And there, with a knife of the
black glass that is found hereabouts ——' He drew the
edge of his pudgy hand dramatically across his throat.

Vensi gave a silent gasp and glanced a question at Father.
His only change of expression was in his eyes, gleaming
with amusement.

But the archaeologist had seen Vensi's quick query,
had sensed Father's amusement. He laughed at Mutz.
'I'll lay a wager you're spoofing me,' he accused him good-
naturedly. He turned to Father. 'Do you speak English
as well as you understand it?' he asked.

Father grunted. 'No. Too much bad,' he replied, exag-
gerating his own deficiencies. He didn't care to traffic
with this *bohanna*, and, besides, there was no use irritating

Mutz twice in one day. Already Mutz's plump face had set as hard as mutton tallow when it cools in a bowl, and only his eyes were lively with malice.

The *bohanna* was not to be so lightly put aside. Probably he liked Father's strong, keen face, Mother's deep, steady glance. Father and Mother stood out in any group, inspiring confidence and admiration.

'You look smart,' said the *bohanna*, 'and you look as if you wouldn't string a fellow, either. When you folks have got your trading done, come on up to my trailer, won't you? I'd like to have you tell me the names of some of the katchina dolls I've been collecting.'

'Boy is alone with sheep,' Father objected.

'I won't keep you long,' the *bohanna* promised. 'Lomavoya,' he said, 'give these kids a quarter's worth of candy and bubble gum on me.' His big high boots carried him in long strides to the door.

Presently Father followed, the hastily purchased box of matches in his hand. That was a wasteful business, squandering a nickel with no eye-shopping, no gossip, to show for it. But the *bohanna's* assurance was like strong ropes pulling the Family after him — and besides, he would perhaps pay.

Mother trudged after Father, the baby-cradle stretching her arms, and Vensi followed, Omva riding in her shawl and the portly paper bag which Lomavoya's clerk had handed her clutched tight.

The crowd of Indian eyes pivoted to see them go, the few children unconsciously moistening their lips as they watched the departure of the candy and gum. Though Vensi's gaze was fixed on Mother's ragged moccasin heels, she could feel those glances, could feel that not all were friendly. Every time Father and Mother lent a hand to the whites some misfortune came. This time perhaps it would be that the Village Council would take part of the

Family away from Father and Mother. Vensi had had
much of the care of Omva. To lose her clinging little arms,
her nestling head, her increasing talk — that would be to
lose a part of Vensi's own self. Today she realized more
keenly than ever before what such a loss would be. And
even in these few short days the boy-baby had grown
precious to her. Yes, life without the babies would lack
a tender sweetness. But if Vensi and Nuva were to be
taken away from the House on Top, then indeed the whole
of life would be broken into small and useless bits.

Now, however, there was nothing to do but follow the
ragged moccasins that followed the ragged moccasins that
followed the great high-laced boots.

It could not be denied that the trailer was interesting.
Packed tight in that small space was more furniture than
in the House on Top and the ranch-house put together.
The *bohanna* lighted a stove that burned the unseen
bohanna fuel, and set coffee to cooking in a glass-roofed
coffee-pot. Mother sat down on the floor with the cradle
across her knees. The boy-baby was fretting, but it was
not time for him to eat; and Vensi guessed that Mother
did not want to uncover him, anyway, because if she did
there would be a lot more talk about albinos and whether
there was any truth in Mutz's made-up stories. Mother
jiggled the cradle to quiet the feeble cry, shifting up one
knee and then the other in practiced fashion, and crooning:
'Go to sleep, my baby! Go to sleep, my baby!'

By the time the *bohanna* had opened a cupboard and
revealed forty — fifty — katchinas, the coffee was shooting
up into its glass roof in a fashion that fascinated Vensi.
She gave only half an ear to their host, until he grumbled
to Father that the natives made him pay through his
nose for some of those wooden dolls. That did seem curious,
and it drew Vensi's attention from the percolator to the
bohanna's beak, nearly as large as Mongwi's. But she was

much too hungry to puzzle over it long. It was past noon, and the Family had not eaten since their scanty breakfast.

The *bohanna* opened a box of thick yellow crackers and an oval tin that let out an unfamiliar smell. He set out a bowl of sugar, and rammed two holes in the top of a can of milk. Then he waved them to eat. Presently they were all munching, and drinking coffee with much sugar and milk, while Father, his voice muffled by food, named the bright-painted katchinas, one by one.

Vensi cautiously tried the strong-smelling canned food and found it not bad, though she looked to Father for explanation.

'It's a kind of pollywog,' he said — 'fish.'

'Fish?' Vensi whispered, and stopped chewing, shifting the morsel to her cheek. Fish were a strange something foreign to the desert. Navajos held them taboo, and even Hopis avoided them.

'It is all right,' Father reassured her. 'You do not need to be so careful when it is *bohanna* food, not Indian.'

Vensi thankfully finished her sardine. It probably would not deepen their ill-luck to enjoy the feast; and it was certainly enjoyable. The *bohanna* even opened a can of tomatoes. The flattened egg of the house-on-wheels grew thick with lovely food-smells. Though it grew also very warm, Vensi was sorry when the *bohanna* stepped around over the Family, opening the windows and pressing a button that made a little fan whirl around. The fan sent the air out the windows in scurrying breezes, so that the lovely food-smells were wasted.

Father named the katchinas, and the white man nodded with satisfaction and checked the list he held, or else shook his head at the list and wrote in new names beside the old ones. Other Hopis, before Father, had given him names, it appeared, and quite likely some of them had given him the wrong ones, as Mutz would have done.

Vensi's eyes strayed from the familiar figures. Thumb-tacked to the walls were paintings of ceremonial dancers, made with exquisite precision on paper that was the color of sand. Nuva, she thought, could have done even better; or at any rate almost as well, if he had had the right brushes and paints and that beautiful sand-toned paper, against which the colors, sharpened with white, burned so bright. The thought of Nuva and his painting made her heart sink again. If anything should happen to take Nuva away from the House on Top and give him to Honawu —! Honawu sneered at Nuva's painting; he would never help him toward his heart's desire.

If anything should happen. But surely this was nothing bad, to name the katchinas. These little wooden dolls were not secret. Every year hundreds of them were made. The katchina-makers carved them, cunningly, from dry cotton-wood boughs and roots, and painted them vividly and decked them with feathers and spruce twigs. Some were given to the children, so that, through them, they should learn to know the spirits of their ancestors, who had in-fluence to make the sun shine and the rain fall and the crops grow. Others — seldom the fine ones — were sold to the traders, who in turn sold them to the tourists. So what was secret or sacred about the names?

Presently Father had told them all: Mother-of-Katchinas, in her lofty terraced headdress, the witch Soyoko and the black-and-gray-striped clowns, the Corn Maiden, and the rest. And the Family had finished off the thick yellow crackers and the sardines and the tomatoes and the coffee and the sugar and the cream and felt much better. They were gathering themselves together and trying to think of a polite way to take their leave when the *bohanna* intro-duced another subject.

'Do you happen to have any old things you'd like to get rid of — sell to the museum?' he asked Father carelessly.

Father's eyes grew opaque. 'Old things? What you meaning, old things? I got no old things only clo'es.' Laughing, he stuck out a ragged moccasin.

The *bohanna* let his careless manner slip. 'I heard you had old clan things,' he said. 'I'll not let on. Nobody around here need know. If they're as good as I've heard they are, the museum will pay you well. And they're yours, aren't they?'

'I got no nothings to sell,' Father repeated stolidly. 'Good-bye.'

He swung himself down from the trailer door, and reached up to take the cradle from Mother. Silently they all crowded out after him, crunching their crumbs underfoot. The *bohanna* sighed explosively.

'Well, thanks for the katchina names, anyway,' he said, shaking Father's hand. 'Where is it you live, my friend? I might be wanting to ask about some more names. I'm leaving Monday, and I've got to finish up.'

'Middle Village,' Father answered. 'Up on Top.'

With a feeling of relief they climbed into their wagon, drawn up in the shade at the side of the trading-post, and drove northward to their ranch. They had shaken off the *bohanna*, and that without any of the lies so hateful to this family — at least without any spoken ones. Certainly they did live in Middle Village, and certainly they lived Up on Top, not down on the ledge. It would be the *bohanna's* own ill-fortune if he went to see them any time before Monday and was met by a padlocked door.

'Silver he gave me, a half-dollar, when he shook my hand,' Father murmured. 'Fat pay for telling him the names of the katchinas.'

'And for filling ourselves with his good food,' Mother added with a twinkle of satisfaction.

'Mutz had told him of the Old, Precious Things: I know it. It was the telling that made Mutz's eyes shine so in

the trading-post,' Father went on with bitter wonder.
'Doubtless he thought to tempt us to do the evil and then,
like enough, spread the news abroad in the village. The
enmity of these men is hard to comprehend.'

'And the *bohannas*, why do they wish to pry into the
secrets of the People?' Vensi murmured.

'That also is hard to comprehend,' Father answered with
a shrug.

'But the Old, Precious Things' — Mother had spoken
up suddenly, in a voice that quavered — 'Sometimes I
have wondered whether they are after all so important to
our clan. Sometimes I have wondered whether they were
so important to anyone.'

While Father and Vensi sat silent with surprise, Mother
went on: 'I can't help puzzling about them. The food
I have carried to them throughout the years, have they
eaten one grain of it all? No, it piles up and piles up before
them. They don't eat!' she said in the low, intense tone
of one who tells at last an astounding secret. 'I think maybe it is like in a book Mees McClung read, they have eyes,
but they do not see, they have ears, but they do not hear;
and they have no heart and no breath, so they cannot eat.
Well, then, why —?'

Father, looking straight ahead, spoke sternly: 'Enough
of that.'

Mother was still, and so the Family rode for a mile or
more. Then Father looked back, with one of his own tender
smiles. 'A candy would taste good, daughter,' he said.

They each took one of the biggest. The large, hard
sweets bulged the cheeks and trickled juicily down the
throats, lasting almost the whole way home. Omva's
trickled down her chin, also; and Vensi found her trying
to give a taste of it to the hungry kid, who had been tied
in the wagon while the Family visited the trading-post and
the house-on-wheels.

Nuva was bringing in the sheep when they reached the ranch-house.

'But where is that Askee?' Vensi wondered aloud.

The big grizzled mongrel was not to be seen. The Family did not ask Nuva about him at once. Father unharnessed the mules and watered them, and Mother took the babies into the house. Vensi went to the corral to help Nuva, handing him, with a smile, the jawbreaker she had saved for him. He tucked it into his cheek. 'Good,' he mumbled, and stationed himself by the gate to count his charges.

'One — two — forty — forty-two ——'
And that was all.

'Brother! What has happened?' Vensi cried. 'Day before yesterday fifty-one and now forty-two! And Askee ——'

Nuva shifted his candy to answer.

'Askee, he is dead,' he answered heavily, 'and nine young ones of the flock, they, too.'

'Nine!' she whispered. 'I knew it would come, the bad luck.'

He turned quick eyes upon her, as he fastened the gate. 'Why?' he demanded. 'Why did you know it?'

'Because of helping the *bohanna* in the house-on-wheels.'

'And how did you help him?'

'Only by telling the names of the katchina dolls. But he is that one who is said to break into the graves of our people and take from them sacred things for the whites to stare at.'

'When?' Nuva queried. 'When did you visit this man?'

'Today, as we came through Polacca.'

Nuva laughed shortly. 'Then the wagon was pulling the mules,' he said. 'The help came after the ill-luck had fallen, not before. It was at break of dawn that I found them dead — lambs, kids, dog.'

Slowly boy and girl went to meet Father at the watering-
trough. There Nuva told the story to both parents, for
Mother, sensing trouble, came out from the house in time
to hear.

Once in the night Nuva had been wakened by Askee's
snarling and barking, he said. He had sat up to listen, but
there was nothing more, only the one barking; so he had
lain down again. But he slept uneasily, and rose as soon
as dawn lightened the windows, hurrying to the corral to
make sure that all was well.

All was not well. Askee was gone, and the coyotes had
again squeezed between the crooked uprights of the wall.
Two kids and seven lambs they had killed and half-
devoured.

'And Askee did not come back?'

Nuva's face went blank with pain. 'Askee could not
come back. Over yonder a little way I found him, where
he had eaten poisoned meat. I did not know there was
poisoned meat anywhere about.'

'Nor did I know it,' Father agreed in the level tone of
trouble. 'The poison called strychnine, some have put out
for the rats and field-mice; and Washindon has also scattered poison for the prairie dogs; but, so far as I knew,
none hereabouts.'

Without more words, he led the mules from the water
and hobbled them to graze.

'*Okiway!*' Mother sucked in the word with a breath and
went back to the house.

'Have you — what have you done with Askee?' Vensi
asked.

Nuva shook his head. 'I left him where he lay. I did
not think that dog would run away from his sheep even if
he did smell meat.'

'Show me,' Vensi said.

Puzzled, Nuva led the way across sandy ripples, where

feet sank deep with each step and with each step must be pulled free.

Vensi did not like to look at old Askee, lying stiff and still, never to laugh again. It was the rope she looked at, stooping with hands on knees, not touching it. When she raised her eyes to Nuva, they were wide and black with surprise.

'The rope,' she said: 'didn't you see that it had been cut with a knife?'

They raced back to the house to tell what they had found. There the little baby was crying, and Mother was pulling everything out of her starch-box cupboard. She turned an anxious face to them when they came in, and with Father she listened to their story.

'That means,' Father said when they had finished, 'that one has fed the dog poisoned meat and then cut the rope and let him stagger away to die.'

'And *that* means,' Mother put in, 'that an enemy has been lurking around, to do this thing; and when our son went to hunt Askee, that one has come in and taken what he could find.'

'Taken?' Nuva and Vensi asked as with one voice. 'Taken what?'

'A sack of white flour,' Mother said in a flat voice; 'and, much worse, the case of milk we had brought for the boy-baby.'

MUCH worse indeed! Already it was well past the time for the boy-baby's evening meal. The sun was about to drop behind the knife-edge of Second Mesa, and at this time of year its position meant half-past six or thereabouts. Besides, the *tiposhoya* himself told the hour, screaming it urgently to a world that did not hurry, as usual, to press the bottle nipple into his open mouth.

Mother and Vensi went scrabbling through every corner and cubbyhole, hoping to find what they knew was not there: a forgotten can of milk. There was nothing.

'The Navajos,' Nuva offered, 'they give the babies coffee in their bottles, if they have nothing better. At least it keeps them alive.'

'At the hospital they said that coffee was very bad for them,' Mother demurred.

'But we must do something,' Father urged, picking up

the cradle and joggling it in his arms. 'My mother used to grind the piki very fine and mix it with water for my smallest brother ... He died, to be sure.'

Momentarily the howling ceased, Father clucked and chirped, and then, as the *tiposhoya* broke into another howl, Father sang loudly.

'The field nurse says that piki is bad for babies because of the wood ashes we use in the batter,' Mother demurred.

'When we had the motherless lambs last summer,' Vensi suggested, raising her clear little voice to a shout above the boy-baby's cry and the man's song, 'I remember what we did. We boiled the fine corn meal and strained it and put it in the milk for them.'

'But where is the milk?' asked Nuva.

'Even in water it would fill his stomach, maybeso.'

'Try it, daughter,' Mother said, making a wry face over the duet and sitting down and taking the cradle on her knees.

The boy-baby's mouth was squarely opened, his eyes squeezed shut, his cheeks pulled full of dimples. His voice had grown stronger, these few days, and he was achieving an amazing squall. 'Ah-way! Ah-waaay!' he shrieked.

Nuva looked at him in pitying amusement. '*Ah-we!*' he joked. 'You must be a Navajo.' *Ahwe* is the Navajo word for 'baby.'

The baby took fresh breath and rose to a new crescendo. If his arms and legs had not been firmly bound he would have been using them to express his hunger and wrath, drawing them up as might a little pink frog. As it was, face and voice had all the work to do. Spurred by their sound and fury, Vensi got the water boiling, and stirred in the flour-like meal with care, so that it should not lump.

'What to strain it through?' she asked uncertainly.

'A piece of cloth,' Mother answered, jouncing the yelling cradle on her knees. 'I think there is a piece of cloth tucked away under the roof-pole in the corner.'

'Cloth must be boiled,' Vensi observed, when she had found the small rag.

'Boiling is for *bohannas*' — Nuva tossed the words scornfully over his shoulder as he departed.

'But when we did not boil, then was when Omva had the sickness,' Vensi called after him.

'*Antsa*, truly,' Mother assented regretfully. 'The *bohannas* must have brought the sickness-bugs, for Grandmother says the Hopis used never to have them. Nor did the Hopi babies have stomachs like *bohanna* clocks, to go off, with a yell, every four hours. Yet now, crazy as it seems, the white ways work with them: they cry less and they grow faster.'

Gruel had never been so slow in the making. The fire smoked and sulked and would not bring the rag to a boil, and, when it did boil, Vensi burned her fingers getting it out of the water.

At last, with her eardrums crackling from the baby's howls, she strained the gruel through the sterilized cloth, squeezing it energetically with the unscalded hand. Miss McClung might not have approved of that unboiled palm, nor the field nurse; but there were limits to endurance.

Next came the difficult process of getting the strained gruel out of the broad-topped bowl and into the narrow-topped bottle. When Vensi had finished, half the gruel was on the outside; but she scraped it off with a spoon and finally had three ounces where it belonged.

By this time the boy-baby was purple, and his voice had screamed itself out of the top of the register until only a faint, hoarse whisper remained.

'Like a small bird he is,' Mother murmured, dancing her knees harder. 'So much must he eat, and so often, to keep the small life burning.'

Vensi was hot and damp and her pulses were jumping, by the time she could sit down on the floor beside his cradle

and poke the nipple into his open mouth. His cry halted in
mid-air, and without opening his eyes he grabbed and sucked
so hard that he almost strangled. Only for an instant. Once
he had tasted the watery stuff he thrust the nipple out again
with an angry tongue and took up his wail where he had
left it.

Mother and Vensi, and even Father and Nuva, turn
about, urged the thin liquid down his small gullet, but an
ounce or two was all they could force him to take.

'We will boil some mutton and give him the broth for his
next feeding,' Mother said worriedly. 'Strong broth, well
cooked down — one would think even a small baby must
get strength from that.'

The fresh fire heated the ranch-house through, and the
boiling mutton filled it with strong steam, but to no avail.
The boy-baby would take less than two ounces of the broth,
and what he did take did not suit his frail stomach, for he
cried convulsively.

The Family went early to bed. Father and Nuva rolled
themselves in their blankets on the ground, one on each side
of the corral, to guard their diminished flock from the coyotes now that Askee was gone. Vensi thought the men had
the better of it. The house was slow in cooling off, and the
baby screamed, though more and more faintly, for hours,
while Omva, wakened by his complaints, yelled in duet
with him. Vensi was always being dragged painfully from
heavy sleep, and plumping back into it when she was re-
leased by an interval of blessed quiet.

Next morning Mother tried straining the gruel into some
of the mutton broth. The *tiposhoya* was not fooled. Ex-
pectantly he took a pull at the nipple, and with an expression of weary disgust he ejected it and gathered his breath
to cry again. And when, toward evening, his hunger drove
him to try even this detestable substitute, new troubles
assailed his nurses. Every two minutes the corn meal

clogged the holes in the nipple, and they must be opened
with a fine hairpin which Mother had by great good fortune
once found and kept. The whole family was exhausted
before sunset.

Father and Nuva had had to go on with the shearing, of
course, but they stopped often between sheep and came,
hot and moist, to the house to listen anxiously to the baby's
weakening cry, and to study his little puckered face, with
the greenish-blue shadow around the mouth.

'He is shrinking again,' Mother told Father on one of
these inspections. 'Look you if he is not shrinking.'

She had his covers off and was rubbing him gently with
grease. Vensi's heart tightened at sight of those mottled
arms and legs, like picked chicken bones. Yesterday,
though you could not honestly call him anything but thin,
you could yet find a muscle as large as a bean in the calf of
each leg. Today these muscles had softened to nothing.

Vensi said suddenly, 'If he — should die, then we should
not only lose the small sweet one, but the Village Chief
and the Council would say ——' The salt tears suddenly
tickled her cheeks.

'They would be glad of any cause for complaint,' Father
agreed somberly. 'But what more can we do? Son, the
flock is bleating. Time, I think, to shut them up for the
night.'

Vensi's eyes suddenly widened with thought. 'Why did
we not think of it?' she cried. 'Milk going to waste, and
none of us ever thinking! And even if we do not like it, the
bohannas say it is good, better than canned milk.'

'The nanny-goats!' Mother ejaculated, lifting her hands
in astonishment. 'It is as if we were Black Mountain Navajos dying of thirst beside one of the white water-troughs.
Water at a turn of the wrist, but we do not know what the
faucet is for.'

'Yes, those whose kids were killed, bleating because they

had no young to suckle, and yet we —! Dezba's family,
they sometimes milk their goats, and if the milk is well
boiled it does not taste so bad, though the flocks are possessed to eat all the strongest-tasting weeds.'

Father's face smoothed with relief, and smile-lines took
the place of his worry-wrinkles. 'It is as the Mission-Marys
are always telling us, we Hopis are bound hand and foot by
past custom. Because it is not custom to use the milk of
animals, we are blind to the possibility. We must learn to
change, and this is a good beginning.'

Almost at once he came leading one of the childless
nanny-goats. Mother left Vensi to lace the baby into his
cradle, and with her usual decisiveness herself sat down on
her heels beside the tied beast. But the decision faltered as
she thrust the clean pan into place and grasped one of the
two long teats. Never had she milked anything, nor even
watched another milk, since the Hopis milked neither
herds nor flocks. And never had Nanny felt a human hand
grasping her so demandingly. With a flurry of small hoofs
she sent the pan clattering, and tumbled Mother in a heap
on the ground.

Mother scrambled up, laughing and scolding, and Father
grasped the goat firmly by the two neat pendants under
her chin, and called to Nuva, who came running, to hold her
hind legs. Thus anchored, she was still, and Mother grasped
the teat again. Nanny twitched and quivered, but nothing
happened.

Vensi had been watching through the open door, tilting
the cradle from side to side in a vain attempt to quiet the
hiccuping cries. Now she called, 'I have watched Dezba.
If we were to give her a very little coarse meal, so that she
would be happy ——'

Mother sat back and brushed the hair from her eyes with
an arched wrist. 'You try it, daughter,' she said. 'Also
try the milking, for your hands are smaller and softer than
mine.'

At first Vensi was no more successful than Mother. She
tried this way and that way, tightening her fingers gently,
without letting the nails touch the tender flesh, and crooning softly as she did so. Anxious as she was, she had all she
could do to sing without laughter, Nuva made such mocking
faces at her songs. She turned her eyes away from him and
persisted; and presently she could feel the twitching gray-
white body relax. Nanny scooped up a mouthful of the
meal with her strong lower teeth and began to chew rhyth-
mically; and then a thin spurt of milk struck the empty can
and played a musical accompaniment to Vensi's croon.
The Family laughed aloud with delight.

They had relaxed too soon. Gnats gathered in a cloud
around the goat, stinging the milker and the milked. Suddenly Nanny kicked vigorously forward at the tormentors,
jerking her leg out of Nuva's grasp and sending the can
flying. With a cry of distress Vensi scrambled to pick it up:
all but a few ounces of the precious liquid had been spilt.

In the end, though, she had a cupful of milk. The whole
family gathered around as Mother strained it through the
gruel rag, boiled it over a quickly coaxed blaze, diluted the
rich white stuff, and added a spoonful of Karo. Next,
slowly, not to waste so much as a drop, she poured it into
the boiled bottles, and cooled one, little by little, with care
lest it break.

Then came the breathlessly awaited moment when Mother screwed the nipple into the now unwilling mouth,
feebly mewing its distaste for anything that might come to
it. A drop trickled over the baby's tongue, and he swallowed, just as he had swallowed Vensi's tear. Nuva laughed
aloud and slapped his thigh in delight. The *tiposhoya's* blu-
ish lips tightened on the rubber and he drank, sucking and
sobbing at once.

That night Mother and Vensi, in the house, slept as
soundly as the men out under the stars. It was a thankful

sleep, for not only was the dear boy-baby saved, but it seemed as if the Family was saved also, from another threat of danger.

And now they had less than two weeks before they must go back on Top to give the little one his Hopi name. The Naming Party was always, without variation, on the child's twentieth day. If he had been the Family's own son, his early weeks would have taken a different course. Then, for each day, Mother would have drawn a line on the wall, five lines on each of the four walls; and during that time neither she nor the child would have looked upon the sun. Never would the *tiposhoya* have traveled to the ranch, to the Canyon, if he had been in the family of his birth. Now it was well that he took so greedily to the goat's milk, so that he might store up energy for still another jaunt before his naming.

Mother and Vensi had only to experiment with the amount of corn syrup, the amount of water, which seemed to keep him comfortable and well. Again the small beans of muscle hardened in his wee calves.

Soon Vensi was milking two goats instead of one, and she and Omva and Nuva were all drinking. They did not like the milk, but in the back of their minds, helping them to persevere with the new food, were the Agent's words: 'We will wait awhile and see.' They longed to grow fat, so that he would think no more of taking them away from their home.

They did not grow fat: Mother said that they never were still long enough. It was true that they were always moving. Omva was like a kitten that chases its own tail if it has nothing else to do, and the big boy and girl were as active.

For Vensi there was always the milking, after breakfast and before supper. She soon worked out a technique. She tied a goat close to a post of the porch, so that it had little leeway, and she gave it a small pan of food. Then she

grasped a hind leg firmly with her left hand while she milked
with the right, meantime singing a song she had learned at
school.

'"Sweet and low,"' Vensi sang softly, and broke off as
the goat wrenched loose its leg and planted a vigorous hoof
in her stomach.

'"Sweet and low,"' she persevered, when she had gathered herself up again. The goat rubbed its head so violently
against the post, to free it of stinging pests, that Vensi was
upset again, while the goat's neat fore-hoofs pawed the
earth and peppered the foamy milk with sand.

Gradually White Nanny grew to be a pet, but Black
Nanny was never docile. As Vensi approached, the goat
reared on her hind legs and pawed the air, her yellow eyes
gleaming and her chin-whiskers wagging. And when Vensi
urged her toward the milking-post, Black Nanny set all
four black hoofs and hunched herself so that Nuva had to
come and push her from behind.

That twice-a-day tussle with the two goats would have
kept Vensi honed down to thinness without all her other
activities. And presently there was a new task: the treat-
ment of the little flock for sore-nose.

Sore-nose was not common in the district, but once before Father's sheep had suffered with it, and so he knew how
to deal with it, and even had, stuck away between roof-
poles and brush, a bottle of the black stuff the Agent had
given him for treating the disorder. Like cold-sores on
human beings, it was; and it made it hard for the animals to
graze.

Nuva and Vensi attended to the doctoring themselves.
It was an exciting task to chase the beasts into corners and
dab their noses with the thick black medicine.

The late May day was hot. Nuva was dressed simply in
overalls and ragged yellow hair-banda, while Vensi wore her
oldest calico, faded and ragged and short.

'You look like a crane,' Mother told her, chuckling. 'You both look as skinny as our sheep do now, with their fleeces off . . . Yes, you look as poor as homeless Navajos.'

They were soon to look like a few more things, besides.

Their patients crowded silently into corners and galloped with lumbering speed out of the way of boy and girl, while the lambs bounded, bleating, after their mothers. Panting and laughing, Nuva and Vensi dashed after them, brandishing their dripping brown swabs and daubing protesting noses whenever they could reach them. In the hot sun the sheep-smell was stifling, but even so the work was half play.

One curly-horned old buck was determined to escape his doctors. This way and that he turned, but Nuva cornered him at last, with Vensi behind the beast to prevent his escape that way. The swab was about to descend when the buck gathered himself together, lowered his powerful head, and came at Nuva so quickly that it was only by a wild leap over the charging animal that he saved himself from the curved horns.

That leap brought the boy crashing into Vensi and knocked her backward into the corral fence. As she went down, his waving swab smacked smartly across her forehead and cheek.

'You look as if you'd been in the mud-fight at somebody's wedding!' Nuva stammered through breathless laughter.

'Yours and Polemana's, probably!' Vensi retorted. 'But never mind! you are going to look like one of those striped clowns!' She twirled her own swab so swiftly around his forehead and cheeks and chest that he was well striped before he could defend himself.

With a shout he brandished his swab at her, and she, aching with laughter, ducked and twisted past him and squeezed through the corral gate with him close on her heels.

Then for the first time the two became aware of an auto-

mobile drawn up before the ranch-house, and of a small man
in breeches, shiny puttees, and Stetson who stood watching
them. It was that symbol of power and fear, Mongwi, the
Agent.

They stopped as if paralyzed. If he was a figure of fear,
they were figures of fun. Grimy and sweaty from their
work, their clothes in rags and their faces and bodies liber-
ally splashed with murky brown, they looked not only ridic-
ulous, but as ill-kempt and ill-fed and ill-bred as any waifs
one could find anywhere.

BEHIND Mongwi, the Agent, the Water-Witch was folding his tall body together to get out of the car. The Water-Witch, it seemed, was inspecting springs and wells, and stopping to visit some of the ranch-houses on his course, and Mongwi had come with him. Vensi thought the men could not have chosen a much worse time. She and Nuva stood digging their toes into the sand and staring intently at the holes they had made.

The Agent was pleasant. He complimented the Family for treating their sheep's ailment so promptly; and he looked with wonder at the thrifty plants that appeared to grow out of clear sand, and at the laborious shelters that had been made for each one. And he admired Mother's basketry.

Mother sat in the shade with her weaving materials laid in wet sand in a canvas beside her, to keep them pliable. She took the end of a fiber in her teeth and stripped it to the right width with deft fingers that had eyes in their tips: the right width, so that the work should be even, and with clean edges, so that there should be no fuzziness

Close beside her Omva sat on her heels, fiddling solemnly
with a basket-center Mother had made for her, from which
the grass and yucca fiber sprayed shaggily.

'So you're going to be a fine weaver like your mother,'
Mongwi said, leaning over to twitch a lock of her shining
black hair.

Omva dropped her head lower and lower over her play-
work, until she quite overbalanced and tumbled in a heap
on the ground.

Mongwi looked also at the boy-baby, and the Family
were thankful that the *tiposhoya* had stopped shrinking and
begun to grow again. Since it was mid-morning, and warm,
Mother had replaced the usual quilt over the cradle-bow
with a piece of cheesecloth the Mission-Mary had once given
her. The flies buzzed noisily around the outside of the filmy
tent, but only one or two had got in, and the baby looked
both comfortable and clean.

'But is it really good for them to be bound so tight and
kept so still?' Mongwi asked the Water-Witch.

'Doesn't seem to do them a speck of harm,' the Water-
Witch said, his lean face laugh-wrinkled, 'except to flatten
their heads so much that some of them look like paper-dolls.
But that's when they're kept too long on the board, I suppose.'

Vensi, listening beyond the corner of the house, wished
someone would tell Mongwi a Hopi saying, 'You can tell
how well a child is loved by the flatness of his head.' Worth
all the bother of keeping them strapped to the cradle, the
Hopis felt, to see them grow so straight of back and limb,
and without sucking their thumbs or scratching their little
faces.

The Water-Witch turned his attention from house to corral. 'Your flock is smaller than when I saw it last,' he said
to Father. 'Now, how is that?'

Father's eyes veiled themselves. 'Last winter six lost in

snow,' he said slowly, speaking in English for politeness to
Mongwi. 'This summer, eleven. Coyotes.'

'But I thought you had an extra good sheep-dog. The
fellow with the Navajo name.'

'Askee, yes. Poisoned meat. Him dead.'

The Water-Witch looked at Father thoughtfully, but
Father said no more.

'The Government,' Mongwi said, 'wants all the flocks
divided again, Yoki. You understand how it is, don't you?
This reservation is so badly overgrazed that floods are
caused by the lack of vegetation. The floods take still more
of the topsoil, and then there are worse floods, and so on and
on.'

Yes, Father had heard about overgrazing, soil erosion.
Well he knew that the millions of tiny sharp hoofs, the
millions of lower teeth that sheared so close, had continued
for centuries, destroying vegetation, loosening the tight
protective fabric of roots, cutting the earth to dust. Once
the land had been rich, the fathers said. In those days
spring had not brought dust storms to waste the soil, and
summer had not brought floods to gouge out new arroyos in
their fury. That was before the sheep which the Spanish
had brought had multiplied. Today they numbered some
three million head, and the range had grown so poor that of
some of it an acre must be allowed to a single sheep, in other
parts anywhere from four to twenty acres.

'You understand, of course, that you will be paid for the
sheep we take,' Mongwi added, answering Father's de-
pressed silence.

Vensi's heart bounced up as she thought of money and
a dress and shiny shoes from the mail-order catalogue. And
then it swooped down again as she remembered how small a
sum Washindon paid for the sheep and goats it weeded out:
a dollar, a dollar and a half apiece. Yet even then, so it was
said, when Washindon butchered and canned, the Indian

mutton cost the Government four dollars a pound before all was done.

Father's thoughts seemed to be running along the same course. 'The money is never so good for us as the sheep,' he said heavily.

Mother, sensing his somberness, introduced a change of subject. 'Will not Mongwi and the Water-Witch sun-mid-dle-eat with us?' was what she asked in Hopi.

Father turned to the men hospitably. 'Sun, him high,' he said. 'Meat is on stove. You eat?'

The Water-Witch spoke quickly and softly to Mongwi. 'Clean, nice folks. We better accept,' he said.

As if he were thinking, '*Clean?*' Mongwi cast a doubtful glance at the daubed and tousled young people. But he nodded and answered: 'Why, yes, thanks. We'd like to.'

Both Vensi and Nuva melted out of sight and scrubbed themselves with vigor at the trough, using sand to scour the brown sheep-medicine stains. When they had got themselves as presentable as they could, Vensi gave Omva a washing that made her wail and kick.

'But, Little Sister, we've got to look clean for Mongwi,' Vensi said passionately. 'We've got to look clean, if we can't look fat.'

Mother had tidily rolled up her bundle of weaving-stuffs and gone at the preparation of dinner. It was a wonderful meal, with twice the usual amount of mutton, three times the beans, and Mother's especially delectable hominy. There was a pile of piki rolls, too; and fresh bread hot from the frying-pan, crisp and lightly browned and bubbly. For each of the children there was a tin cup of goat's milk: Mother meant to show Mongwi whether or not they were fed on husks. And for a final touch, Father fetched in a double handful of new onions, shining green and white. He had just pulled them, and washed them at the trough before he brought them in. They were as fine as bouquets, laid at intervals along the oilcloth where everyone could reach them.

Mongwi tried a little of this and a little of that, and wound up by eating heartily of everything. On the whole, his chance visit was not a bad thing. It would have been wholly good if he had not caught the boy and girl so dirty and so ragged.

— And if they had not been still so thin! Vensi looked disapprovingly down at herself: the shape of Father's spinning-stick, she was, and not much bigger. When Mongwi had gone, she peeked at her face in the fragment of looking-glass that Mother had set into the adobe plaster of the wall. Her hair, washed often and with good yucca root, was black and glossy as a crow's wing, and below it her eyes shone dark and soft. A faint stain of iodine could still be seen on cheek and brow, but the scouring with sand had brought up the rose-red color to distract attention from the stains.

'Thin! So skinny!' she said breathlessly, when Nuva caught her studying herself.

'Very pretty girl!' he hooted; and she ran away, giggling.

But anyway, she comforted herself, Mongwi ought to see that she was healthy in spite of her thinness, a girl with such very red cheeks.

9.   THE OLD, PRECIOUS THINGS

FOR a while now the Family had no time to consider the Agent's thoughts or doings, or whether the Village Council and Uyi, its Chief, could find excuse to take action against them, or how they would get along with their flock once more divided. For this was the boy-baby's eighteenth day, and on his twentieth he must be named. Abraham Lincoln was the finest possible *bohanna* name; but his real name would be Hopi.

Early in the morning of his nineteenth day the Family drove back to Middle Village, Nuva herding the sheep across the desert as before.

There was much to do on Top. Tawamana, Singing-Girl, and other clan-relations took all the boy-baby's clothes and washed them in accordance with custom. They did not take them down to the Government Day-School and wash them in the laundry tubs there, like ordinary clothing. No, the baby's things must be cleansed with pomp and ceremony at one of the prescribed springs.

In the meantime, Mother and Vensi turned the house inside out, spreading blankets and sheepskins and quilts on Tawamana's roof before their door to sun and air, and cleaning the floor as thoroughly as they could without giving it a fresh coat of clay. There was not time to do that.

Grandmother had come early, bringing an arm of mutton to make the stew, and juniper to make the tea, and good white meal to make the *pikami*, the corn pudding, and pounded yucca root for the bathing and hair-washing.

It was good to be with Grandmother. She was Father's mother, and her face had something the strong kindliness of his: a comely face, not so deeply wrinkled as most of the old women's, but pleasantly plump in the frame of white hair that hung smoothly coiled over her shoulders.

Grandmother grumbled good-naturedly when she found Mother and Vensi sweeping.

'No right Hopi ways left,' she said. 'Never would I have swept away the dirt like that, when I was young.'

Vensi smiled at her as she bent double over her handleless broom. She had heard all this before.

'It's the children that make the dirt, isn't it?' Grandmother demanded. 'Well, then, when you sweep it out and throw it away, aren't you really throwing away the little children?'

'But the teachers say,' Vensi murmured, 'and so do the nurse and the Mission-Mary — they say that dirt is — dirty.'

Grandmother laughed. 'The world is changing fast,' she said. 'The Hopis, they sat here in the desert for a thousand years, maybeso, without bothering to change. Why should they change? Were not the ways of the People good? And then came the *bohannas* and — pouff! they turned everything upside down, from our housekeeping to our religion.'

Grandmother glanced sharply at her daughter-in-law as she said the word.

'I have not been washed with the white religion,' Mother defended herself. 'Yet I often wonder ——'

Grandmother seemed to understand the unfinished sentence. Her eyes softened into something almost wistfulness, and she glanced over her shoulder and spoke in a lower tone.

'When first I heard the story of the white God,' she said, 'I thought it would do something for me. I thought life would be changed. But I was afraid to step out and declare my belief. If I took the White Way, the old men said, they would cast a death-charm upon my babies, Yoki and the others. And all did die except Yoki. So I was afraid. And now it is too late. Now the story does not stir me as it did when I was young; and, besides, I see many *bohannas* that are worse than the Hopis ——'

Mother looked quickly, anxiously, at Vensi, and turned the talk to matters of the Naming. And presently Vensi missed her, and found her moccasins standing empty in the storeroom, at the entrance to the sacred chamber. Toeing in, they stood, as Mother had stepped out of them, and with their high tops leaning limply toward each other.

Then Vensi knew that Mother was afraid, as Grandmother had been, and was hastening back to look to the Old, Precious Things, to see that no ill had befallen them during her absence. Yet when, presently, Mother was about her work again, Vensi found in her face no peace. Rather, she found a gray pallor and a shine of sweat. But Mother went on at the day's tasks without remark.

All that afternoon came visitors to the House on Top, women clan-relations for the most part. Each brought gifts, basket-trays piled with corn meal or piki and the like. It was a day rich in talk and sociability, but not half so important as the next morning would be.

Throughout the night Vensi kept waking, fearful that the Family would oversleep and be late with the needful preparations. Each time she roused she would listen for

Mother's breathing. Sometimes it would tell her that
Mother slept; sometimes that Mother, too, was awake;
sometimes the deep sleep-breath would be broken by the
silence of rousing. Then Vensi would whisper, 'Is it time?'

Mother would look out at the sky to see which stars
were framed in the peephole above the grinding-bin and
which in the other windows, and she would whisper back,
'Go to sleep: it is a long while yet,' or 'It is awhile yet,' or
'It is a little while yet.'

When at length Vensi was jerked wide awake by the
noise of stirring in the dark room, it did not seem possible
that after so many useless wakings the long-awaited day was
really come.

The Family had scarcely time to make themselves ready
before men and women began to climb their ladder and let
in the morning twilight and the fading stars and the cool,
sweet air before the dawn. The ceremonies began. First of
all, Grandmother uncoiled Mother's hair and washed it well
in a bowl of suds from the yucca root she had pounded yesterday, the old men taking their turn at scrubbing the shiny
black mass with an ear of corn dipped in the suds. Then
Mother was bathed with the juniper tea that steeped on the
hearth, and purified by the juniper steam for the task of
rearing the new child.

After that, Grandmother took the handleless broom and
swept up a handful of the tracked-in dirt on the floor.
Out on the terrace she carried it, on the roof of Tawamana's
house, and flung it abroad, toward mesa and plain. Sikatsi
went with her and flung a dipperful of water after the dirt,
murmuring as she threw it, 'Clouds and rain!'

For some minutes a small scolding had sounded from the
tiposhoya's cradle. It was not yet his eating-time, but the
stir and confusion had disturbed him. Now Grandmother
lifted him out of his blankets and bathed him in the yucca
suds. It was his first water bath, though if he had not been

so small and frail he would long ago have been so bathed,
and rubbed with wood ashes besides, to make his little body
always smooth and hairless. As it was, he was still a frail
petal, and Vensi hardly knew whether to laugh or cry as
she watched Grandmother lower him into the water.

Carefully as she let the tiny body down into the warm
liquid, the *tiposhoya* caught his breath and opened his eyes
wide with fright when he felt this new element. His soft
arms and legs shot out convulsively and then doubled themselves against his body.

He can't get his breath, the poor baby! Vensi thought pity-
ingly as he fought for air. In another instant he had filled
his lungs and was roaring lustily with shock and protest.
Vensi clenched her hands till the nails bit her flesh, she so
longed for the warm pleasure of clasping him close and comforting him.

This was the worst he had to bear, for Mother had refused
to let the hot pitch be touched to his forehead as the custom
was. His roars soon died down to a gentle whimper, and the
women laughed with relief and murmured together in that
high tone that was like the sun song of basking hens. Grandmother laughed, too, but she hurried. This was a show that
must go exactly according to schedule, for the curtain rose
on time, no matter where the players might be.

Father was on the housetop, ready to give the signal when
that curtain was about to come up: Grandmother must work
fast. She rinsed the complaining baby with clear water, and
then dipped a long and perfect ear of corn into a bowl of
corn meal and dusted him with it. She waved the ear at
baby and at mother, and, waving, she prayed: 'May you
live to be old! May you have good corn! May you keep
well! And now I name you Nuvalangpu, Snowball.'

Rapidly the guests gave other names: all relating in some
way to their fathers' clans. Most of the names the baby
would lose as he walked through life, but one, connected
with his own foster-father's clan, he would keep.

Carefully he was laced into his fresh, clean cradle, while
Grandmother sprinkled corn meal in a path to the door. It
was time. Father was leaning over from the housetop, sig-
naling that the sun was about to rise.

That was the thrilling moment, when they all crowded
out upon the terrace behind Grandmother and the baby.
All the women were wrapped in clean *mantas*, and the breeze
that blows at sunrise was cool and new.

Off to the east the earth-edge was cut by the thinnest
knife-blade of flame. As the blade widened and the sky
grew rosy, Grandmother flung back the blanket from the
boy-baby's face and held him out toward the red sun. Corn
meal she held before his whimpering little mouth. Then,
with a prayer, she flung the meal out toward the sun. The
ceremony was finished.

The company trooped into the house, ready for the feast.
Hunger was sharp within Vensi, and she was glad when they
sat down on the floor with the full dishes of food around
them. Laughter and chatter eddied around the pale-haired
tiposhoya; and he seemed well content, now that warmed
and sweetened goat's milk flowed in a comfortable stream
down his small throat.

Almost everything was good. Honawu was at the feast,
to be sure, his presence casting its usual crooked shadow
over the Family's spirits. Besides, he had stood looking at a
picture which Mother had fastened to the wall, and he had
laughed and said: 'The boy has too strong a hand and too
fleet a foot to be playing with paints and paper. It would
not be hard, I think, to get him interested in matters more
manly.'

And his words, somehow, made his shadow darker. It
was almost as if Honawu, peering crookedly up at that
painting of Corn Rock, were gloating over riches already in
his hand.

Still another uneasiness lay heavy upon Vensi. Now

and again she looked at Mother. Sometimes Mother was talking, sometimes smiling, and sometimes, with a set pallor, she was looking inward. But whatever she was doing, Vensi felt sure that all was not well with her.

'Our mother, have you pain?' she asked her, when all the guests were gone. 'No? Well, then, is it the whirling of the head?'

Mother answered, 'No ... No ... No, my daughter, I am quite well.'

It was not until that night that Vensi learned the reason for her mother's pallor and for her inward gaze.

Dark had scarcely fallen when the door of the House on Top was closed and the floor was covered with six bundles which were the Family. They were all thoroughly tired, and Vensi dropped to sleep at once. What had wakened her she did not know: perhaps an ember snapping, or the baby fretting, or Omva calling out; or even — she thought of this later — the footsteps of someone tiptoeing across Tawamana's housetop to the door of the House on Top. Whatever the sound had been, it was not repeated, and while Vensi was struggling back toward sleep again, she heard Mother's voice, soft and low.

'The *bohanna* in the house-on-wheels,' Mother asked, 'did he go back to his own place as he said he would?'

There followed a brief silence, as if Father were surprised by the question, and maybe only half awake. 'I have heard that he went back as he said he would,' Father answered, yawning deeply.

'And you — always since we went from the mesa, when the *tiposhoya* had but a few days, always you have been near at hand, where my eyes at any moment could find you.'

Vensi saw the bundle that was Father bend as he rose on his elbow. His head was a black shape against a gray window.

'What is this you are saying?' he demanded in an astonished tone. 'And to what end?'

Mother caught her breath and her voice was a gasp of pure terror. 'They will say, when they find it out, they will say that we have sold the Old, Precious Things to the evil *bohanna*. You will see. They will make it a reason to take the good fields from us. They will make it a reason to give even our children to others.'

'*What is this that you are saying?*' Father repeated hoarsely. 'Surely you are sleep-talking. The Old, Precious Things stand in their safe chamber. This very day you went in to them.'

Vensi, trying to keep her heart from beating and her breath from sounding, so that she could catch these puzzling words — Vensi heard Mother draw a sharp breath like a sob.

'I went in, yes,' said Mother. 'But they were not standing in that safe chamber. They were vanished.'

10. LIKE TAKING OFF TIGHT SHOES

'THEY were vanished.' If Mother had said, 'All our flock
has fallen dead,' the words would not have been so terrible.

Father was for a moment silent after she had spoken.
Then he said slowly: 'It is not long since you thought these
gods of little power, these precious things of little worth.
Why, then, do you make so bitter an outcry over their
loss?'

In all Vensi's years she had never before heard Father or
Mother doubt one another. Yet doubt surely lay in Father's
query, as doubt had lain in Mother's. It was clear that this
realization came upon Mother, also, for when she replied her
voice was broken as with crying.

'*Okiway!*' she whispered. 'That you and I should question one another. After thirty years together ——'

Vensi took comfort in the thought that Father reached
over, then, and laid a gentle hand on Mother. Nothing
could be worse than that there should be unhappiness between one's parents.

'I think an enemy has done this thing,' Father said at

length. 'That, or else the gods are indeed angry with us,
and have taken back their visible presence.'

'However it has come about, it is a heavy ill to befall
us.'

'*Antsa*, verily. If we were to have a dance to propitiate
the powers ——' Father suggested.

'Our stock of corn is already low,' Mother objected. 'If,
after we had spent it on them, they did not come to our aid,
then what should we do?'

'There will soon be the wool money' — Father spoke of it
with a noticeable hesitancy.

'For Honawu to take from you on your gambling debt'
— Mother did not say it crossly, or even too patiently, but
as to a beloved son who has a weakness. Father's weakness
was gambling. It was a weakness he had in common with
many other Indians; and, to be sure, it had been long since
he had yielded to it. The debt to Honawu was old, and it
was doubtful, besides.

'Crooked playing,' Father muttered. 'Honawu plays all
matters crookedly.'

'But the trouble is to prove it,' Mother said somberly.
'As for the dance, if we were to spend all we have on it,
who knows whether it would serve any purpose? And then
our children must go hungry and ragged next winter.'

'If they are not taken from us entirely,' Father assented.
'And these children have become a part of ourselves, as
much as if they were those three who were born to us in our
youth, and who went away from earth before they had
looked upon the sun.'

'I should not care to live without these young ones,'
Mother said with a half-sob.

Vensi lay stiff in the darkness, and the tears ran down her
face. She thought that Nuva, on the other side of Father,
was probably lying awake also. She thought that her parents probably did not care if she and Nuva did hear; either

they did not care, or else their hearts were so full of pain that they forgot the possibility of being overheard.

Of all this, nothing was said next day. It was as if the night had devoured the words spoken. Yet there remained a cloud of fear because the Old, Precious Things were no longer housed beneath the roof of the House on Top, and a cloud of sadness because between Father and Mother there had been doubt.

Moved by their unease, they made all the more haste to return to the ranch that day. Hurriedly, on the way down, Father visited his apricot tree and mended its screen of brush. Hurriedly he swung out on a side road to his peach trees, which nestled in a saucer of sand on the mesa-side. The sand had blown in around the trees' feet and up to their ankles. It would soon reach their knees if it were not shoveled away. Father took time to shovel it away, for peaches were important to the Hopi diet. They were one of the gifts that had come, centuries ago, from the Spanish, along with sheep and burros and horses and grapes.

It was good to get back to the ranch; like taking off tight shoes, or like getting out into the open from a hot kiva. Here the Family were far from the gloating enmities of Honawu and Mutz, and far from the house which was empty of the Old, Precious Things, and far from those minutes of doubt.

The days passed swiftly, filled with plenty of work. The beans speedily poked themselves up into the light, tender leaves folded between the two halves of each. As soon as that happened, the plants must be shielded with their individual sand-guards of brush or stone, as had been the early corn. Then, too, both corn and beans must be sprinkled, for worms were bad.

Mother had seldom an idle moment; if her hands were free from other tasks she took up her basketry. Even Father used his spare time for handwork. He hung his loom in the

shade of the porch roof and worked on his chief's blanket,
with its stripes of red and white and black.

As for Vensi, when she had nothing else to do, she went
far afield to gather greens; or helped Mother find dyestuffs
and make the dyes. And she was working seriously at
basketry. She had played at it since she was a baby, as
Omva did now, sitting solemnly on her heels so close to
Mother's arm that she hindered her movements; and for
several years she had been making plaques that were good
enough so that Lomavoya was willing to take them in
trade; but Mother usually had made the hardest part for
her: the tight little snail that was the beginning. Now Vensi
set herself seriously to attain perfection — a neat, close
center and even coils and invisible stitches like Mother's.
She even set herself to master the eagle design, and sometimes she worked for hours on it, until her back and fingers
were cramped. Then, when she could stand it no longer,
she would leap to her feet and jog across to a melon patch
of Father's a mile away, Omva on her back. Or she would
ride one of the mules to the field of late corn over near
Pointed Butte.

Nuva had his herding to do, and often he took along his
rabbit-stick, the Hopi boomerang, and brought down a
tasty rabbit or prairie dog with it. It was the best rabbit-
stick on the mesa, he boasted, flying strong and true to its
target. Father had used it in his own boyhood, and when
its stout oak had split on a rock he would not give it up, but
wired it so securely that it had held firm all these years.

The babies were both prospering. The *tiposhoya* ate and
slept and slept and ate. Father made him a crib from a
wooden box, hanging it by ropes from the roof poles, and the
boy-baby laughed and cooed if someone gave it a push
and sent it swinging. And when Mother spread a quilt on
the floor and laid him on his stomach there, to rest him
from cradle-board and swing, he lifted his heavy flaxen

head strongly, rearing up his chest and shoulders as if he were about to creep, and laughing at the pet kid, which Omva had lugged over and dumped in front of him.

So when the Fourth of July rolled round, there were several good reasons why the Family should go to the celebration at First Mesa, and no good reasons why they should not. Father had a fine blanket and Mother and Nuvensi several baskets to take to the trading-post, along with the wool, which had not yet been sold. Lomavoya was offering many prizes for the races and the other events; and besides these attractions the day always gave an opportunity to meet old friends from other villages. Mother's brother did not care to go to the celebration, and was quite willing to herd Father's sheep with his for that day. And the boy-baby was grown strong enough so that the jaunt would not harm him.

So the team of gray mules set out early on the morning of the Fourth, and reached First Mesa before the sun was high.

COMING from the still emptiness of the desert morning into the color and confusion of the celebration almost took Vensi's breath away. The open flat beside the trading-post reminded her of nothing so much as a picture Nuva had once drawn, and which Omva had found and scrawled over with every crayon in the box.

Against the background of store and houses and stone wall moved a rainbow of bright hues; and the wind rushed here, rushed there, tossing handfuls of sand that blurred the scene just as Omva's dirty little fingers had smudged the picture.

Among the wagons drawn up around the big square were a few Navajo outfits, a little aloof, because of the age-old enmity between the two tribes. Dezba's family was among them. Her mother, a tall, lean, commanding woman, had fastened a cedar tree to the wagon-bed to make a shade from the hot sun. Between its branches Dezba grinned

shyly at Vensi, and Vensi made a small motion of greeting
with her hand.

Government people were there, also: teachers, and the
Water-Witch's workers, nurses and doctors and people
from Mongwi's office. Nowadays you could not get away
from the whites. They trickled in everywhere. Most of
them were taking pictures. The Tribal Council could not
stop their cameras here, though they did stop them Up on
Top.

But the greatest part of this picture was made up of
Hopis: Hopis from First and Second Mesas and a few from
Oraibi. They almost blotted out the whites and the Navajos, and because they were so greatly in the majority they
could give themselves over to fun without self-conscious-
ness. They laughed much over little, shouting at each
other while they waited for the day's events to begin. The
would-be contestants and the judges and the general man-
agers knotted in little groups and tried to get things started,
while Lomavoya stood benignantly above the crowd on the
store steps.

Vensi did not mind the delays, there was so much to see:
Polemana's new clothes, and the much jewelry that had
come out of pawn since shearing-time, and how the babies
were growing, and the wonderful way Miss Rivers, the
woman in Mongwi's office, had her red hair rolled and
waved like molded and painted pottery.

Nuva idled along the line of horses drawn up at the
starting-line ready to race, and spoke with the young men
and boys negligently sitting their mounts. Vensi's eyes slid
after him. He might not much mind his ragged overalls
and patched shirt; not even when he noticed Wiki's high
store boots, stitched in flower patterns. But he could not
help minding it that he had no horse; no horse to slouch
arrogantly on now; no horse to send stretching out long to
victory in the races. It was well, she thought, that he was a

fleet runner. Unless there was some unknown entry, he
could win the kick-stone race and the dash, and so get
enough 'tin' — trade tokens — for new trousers.

At last the little knots of arguers dissolved. The line of
horsemen straightened. A pistol-shot snapped it loose.
Straight out across the sand the horses dashed, sending
dogs and children scurrying to shelter. The course was a
mile long, and while a few watchers climbed housetops or
went panting up the Hill-Where-We-Spread-Our-Rabbit-
Skins, to keep the vanishing puffs of dust in sight, most of
them turned their attention to the next event. It was the
baby race, for children under three years.

Father carried Omva out and set her down, paralyzed to
silence, among the other toddlers. The rest of the Family
settled itself to watch. Nuva swung his long legs over the
edge of the wagon-box, the ends of his banda blowing out
like yellow ears, and cheered Omva. Mother sat on the
ground in the shade of the wagon, the *tiposhoya's* cradle
across her lap, well shielded from the dust that whirled and
darted around the open flat. Vensi stayed inside, peeping
out under the partially rolled-up canvas: she liked it better
there. Before the baby race began, the horses came whirling back, streaked with sweat, and now they stood flipping
their tails at flies, laying back their ears at each other,
alongside the Family wagon. And among them was Wiki,
Honawu's sister's son, on his short-tempered cayuse. Wiki
was forever yanking the scrawny scarred beast around so
that he, Wiki, could peer at Vensi under the broad brim of
his Stetson, and the cayuse was forever irritably dancing
back to squeal and nip at a neighboring roan.

Meanwhile the race-track, half veiled by blowing sand,
was as confused as a chicken-yard when a pan of corn has
been thrown in. It was hard to tell who were the contestants, for fathers and mothers, brothers and sisters, ran in
from the edges to start their entries over again or to urge

them on; and even the mounted youths shouted and whistled at their favorites; for Hopi boys liked babies and were not ashamed to show their liking.

Some of the small racers stood stock-still and howled with fright, while others stuck thumbs in mouths and watched their rivals with calm interest. Father reached over and gave Omva a gentle spank when it was time to start, and then stepped out of her sight. Omva rocked back on her moccasin heels and gazed around her with growing alarm, hunting for her people.

Fortunately, the course of the race lay toward the wagon, and, seeing this, Vensi forgot her fear of strangers, forgot even Wiki's bold stare, and clambered out on the wagon's edge beside Nuva, where the baby could see them if she looked up. There Vensi balanced, waving her shawl. She could not bring herself to call, but Nuva shouted for them both: 'Come, Little One! Come running, Little Sister!'

Omva was making up her face to roar, when she heard the familiar voice and, looking up, saw the familiar red-and-black-checked shawl. At the reassuring sound and sight her baby puckers cleared and she started ahead, stretching both hands behind her in a funny way she had, and plunging onward with eyes for nothing but the Family.

Midway of the course she tripped and fell headlong. Vensi scrooged herself into a knot of eagerness and Nuva grew hoarse with shouting encouragement. The baby girl scrambled to her feet and trotted on, her sand-pricked hands spread wide like starfish.

Next she had a collision. The speediest little boy had got sand in his eyes and had reversed his course without a traffic signal, paddling back toward the starting-point with howls of protest. He and Omva smashed head-on. Again Omva scrambled up and onward.

When she reached the finish-line she had worked up her best speed, a hop with one foot and a trot with the other.

She did not pause for the tape: she did not even see it. It caught her knees and pitched her across itself ahead of all comers. On her stomach she skimmed over the sand, flying along beside the Family's wagon amid widespread applause and laughter.

Laughter and applause were short-lived. Cheering changed to shouts of warning. Wiki's cayuse had circled out away from its roan neighbor's bared yellow teeth, and its heels were whirling straight toward Omva.

Swallowing a cry of terror, Vensi was over the wagon-edge; but Nuva was ahead of her. He seemed to pluck the baby sister in full flight, himself crashing into the cayuse's flank.

He limped back to the wagon and handed Omva up to Vensi, muttering that he was all right. There was nothing for Vensi to do but stumble up to the judges and receive Omva's prize for her, blushing and hiding her face desperately in the little winner's sand-gritty hair.

The prize was 'tin' for fifty cents, and Omva would neither take it nor look at it. She still held out her soft palms, pitted and red with sand, and her breath caught in small sobs of fright and hurt.

'This will buy you a little bracelet, Baby Sister,' Vensi whispered comfortingly, as she set her down beside Mother and the *tiposhoya*.

Since mid-morning the wind had been more or less sportively threatening the festivities, grabbing at broad-brimmed hats and ballooning Navajo skirts and throwing sand into everybody's eyes. Now it swept across the open ground, shrieking, and with it came a sudden patter of rain. The horses danced nervously, and women scurried to shelter. It seemed the proper time to declare a recess for dinner.

Half the spectators swarmed over to the church, which crouched in a rich shade of cottonwood trees between the mission and the Water-Witch's house. The Mission-Marys

had invited not only the little band of church members,
here and at the other mesas, but everyone else who cared to
come. So the Family carried their food and their babies up
the sandy hill, knowing that Miss McClung would be there,
and other acquaintances besides.

They found the Mission-Marys and some of the Hopis
skittering around, bent double against the dusty-smelling
shower to protect the picnic, which they were carrying from
the scant shelter of the trees into the church itself. Father.
helped the other men push the pews to one side, and the
women spread mission tablecloths and Indian oilcloths and
canvas end to end in a hollow square on the floor-space that
was left. Baskets and pails, tin cups and plates, were
thumped down on the floor-table, and a hundred Indians
eased down around them. Miss McClung and the First
Mesa Mission-Marys had set two tubs of lemonade and a
boilerful of coffee on the platform, and there was an unend-
ing procession of Hopis tiptoeing over and around the eat-
ers, with hot tin cups and cold tin cups.

It was good to come in out of the dusty heat and the
dusty deluge, into the coolness of the church-house. Heat
had prickled out in Vensi's neck and stuck her dress to her
shoulder blades. The church had thick Hopi walls against
the heat, and the breeze through its doors made damp clothing refreshingly cool. Vensi, safe between Father and
Mother, and with Omva's wants to attend to so that she
need not talk — Vensi liked being here. She flashed a silent
smile at Miss McClung when that Mission-Mary halted
before the *tiposhoya*, her hands full of dishes, and exclaimed: 'Well, good gracious, how the little snipe has
grown! And how cunning he is, bless his little heart!'

Vensi liked being here, though it was strange, she
thought, that the *bohannas* wished the house of their god
to be so starkly white. There was a clear cleanness about
the little place that was not bad, only too much. Two

splashes of color it held and two alone: a finely woven scar-
let-and-white Hopi blanket on the pulpit, and one window
of bright stained glass. Vensi, eating little bundles of blue
mush boiled in wrappings of corn husk, and drinking the
cold, sweet lemonade — Vensi thought vaguely that if she
had all the money in the world, like *bohannas*, she would
hang colored pictures on every one of God's walls, and
spread colored blankets on His floor, besides.

The rainstorm beat itself out quickly, doing little more
than lay the dust. It was over and done and the sun shining
before the slow-eating Hopis were through their food and
visiting. Father shook his head in disappointment when
they came out and saw the sand already dry again. The
fields had got little benefit.

The children sang 'America,' and Miss McClung led
them in a salute to the flag. She had a brand-new trimming
for that salute. All year she had saved paper sacks, big and
little, and persuaded her friends to save them. She had
enough for every man, woman, and child at the picnic, and
she explained, with her own energetic brand of illustration,
how to blow them up and twist the tops tight. The minute
the salute was done, she gave the signal, and each right fist
burst each inflated bag. That scattering and windy bang
was the only 'fireworks' of the day.

Now the Hopis were straggling back to the trading-post.
A girls' race was announced as first for the afternoon, a relay, with the course over the Water-Witch's hill, past the
peach orchard, to Red Earth — where the Hopis got the
red clay for their house plaster.

Dezba was still sitting under her portable cedar tree, and
she came over to the Family's wagon, walking in the proud,
shy way of Navajo girls, with nothing of her moving but
her feet, and her skirts floating around them. She stood
looking up at Vensi. 'You run good,' she said. 'Come, be
on my side.'

Vensi shook her head. Each girl on the winning side
would get maybe a twenty-five-cent trade token. The next
girls' race paid better, for the first prize was a dollar. A
dollar would buy enough goods for a dress. If Vensi could
force herself to brave all those staring eyes, she would run
in the next race.

As she watched the relay racers, she was glad she had not
joined them. Polemana was among them, in a flower-garden
print, clear and new, and with striped anklets and stylish
oxfords. Dezba, poised at the starting-line, wore a basque
of wine-colored velvet. It was buttoned all the way down
the front with silver shells, and the turn-over collar had
corners of wrought silver. As Dezba flew past the other
racers, her black sateen skirt billowed out over an opulence
of other skirts, red and checked and yellow. Vensi pulled
her summer shawl closer, hot though the day, to hide her
patched and faded dress.

Mother, too, hid herself in her shawl, and Vensi took note
that she had turned its worst rags carefully inside. Mother's dress was washed almost to whiteness, and she had
not an ounce of silver to save her pride. She, too, shook her
head when her race was announced, the women's race.
Vensi was sure that Mother half-wanted to run. Like other
Hopis, she enjoyed play and laughter, and she was so much
thinner than most of the women that she would have stood
a good chance of winning the dollar in trade.

Vensi thought that it was not Mother's shabbiness that
prevented her so much as the thread of unfriendliness that
seemed to run through the crowd, her face was so sober as
she watched the line of racers. Everyone else was laughing
as the women puffed and panted and waddled along the
course: Mutz's wife, the fattest woman on Second Mesa,
and Tawamana, and Sikatsi, and Honawu's Lenmana, very
dressy, with even her wife-locks cut in an elaborate curve
across her moon-cheeks.

Next would come the boys' foot-race; already the contestants were making ready for it, behind the trading-post.
Vensi looked in surprise at Nuva. He had counted on this
contest, for he could run with the long, easy motion of a
greyhound Vensi had once seen, as if it were no trouble at
all. But now he shook his head and twitched an explanatory
chin down toward his knee.

'I stepped wrong when I caught Little Sister,' he said.

So that race was out. It had been bad enough for him to
stand by, mountless, when the other boys sat their horses
in arrogant ease, proud of their animals and some of them
proud also of gaudy shirts and broad-brimmed hats and
cowboy boots. It had been bad enough to watch from the
ground as they dashed by in a haughty whirl of dust. But
now to have to forego the foot-race, besides, in which he
could have retrieved his pride while he won a dollar in trade!

At least, Vensi thought, Wiki would not win. She did not
want him to win anything, she thought, not anything at
all, though maybe that was unkind of her. Standing im-
portantly there in his running-trunks he looked like a
lumpy doll the children might have made out of clay and
sticks. Nothing about his face or body had the clean-cut
strength and firmness of Nuva's.

Then came the girls' second race, and Dezba beckoned
Vensi in the Navajo way, with outthrust lips like the cari-
cature of a kiss, and tossed-back head.

'Why not, my daughter?' Mother asked, as Vensi hesi-
tated. 'If you were to get the dollar and buy the gingham, I
would make it into a pretty school dress for you.'

Vensi pictured the school dress. It would not be smartly
styled, but it would be bright and fresh. She knew the bolt
of goods on Lomavoya's shelf, a red-and-white plaid; and
she had red buttons that had been on a dress she had worn
when she was small: in the bottom of Mother's box in the
storeroom those buttons waited, under the clothes for the

ceremonials. She could feel the crisp newness of the skirt under her brown fingers as she swished into school wearing it; she could smell the smell of new cotton. Thinking of it, she threw off her shawl and made a convulsive motion toward the wagon-edge.

'Good!' Nuva murmured without looking her way.

Then her heart swelled and crowded suddenly into her mouth. Against Lomavoya's wall lounged Wiki, and his eyes were upon her. She clutched the shawl back around her shoulders and crouched low in the security of the wagon. Inside that wagon were comfort and dearness, outside everything she feared, all wavering together in the hot brightness.

Dezba won the race, with Honawu's girl second. Nuva snorted. 'You could have beaten them both,' he muttered over his shoulder to Vensi.

Miss Rivers, the red-haired white woman from Mongwi's office, had been sauntering from wagon to wagon, talking with the English-speaking Indians. Now she came up to the Family.

'I hear you hurt your knee when you rescued your little sister,' she said to Nuva. 'I hope it's nothing serious.'

'Not bad,' he said, unsmiling.

'I'm glad this sweet baby girl is safe,' Miss Rivers went on, touching Omva's dimpled hand with the tip of a polished fingernail. Omva drew back her hand, staring in fascination at the shining nail.

'And the other baby,' Miss Rivers went on, 'my word, but he's growing. Hello there, Abraham Lincoln!'

'Even you, Vensi' — she turned her attention to the girl, who was silently watching her — 'even you have grown some; I began to think you never would. When are you coming to see me again?'

Once, to her mingled terror and delight, Miss Rivers had called her in to dinner at her small house at the Canyon.

She had been kind to Vensi: too kind, as if she would like to
be inside Vensi's mind, finding the self that hid there.
Vensi could not think how to answer her invitation now.
She was spared the necessity, and by Honawu, who had
sauntered up and stood listening.

'Nice girl — no?' he remarked genially to Miss Winters.
'Growing up. Soon marrying some good Hopi boy with
plenty sheep — no?'

Vensi shivered, knowing what Hopi boy he had in mind.
Miss Rivers shivered, too.

'Much, much too young for such notions,' she declared,
surveying Honawu with distaste and drifting on to watch
the burro race, with a dozen shaggy small Hopis struggling
to saddle a dozen shaggy small beasts, before riding them to
the Water-Witch's gate and back, and then unsaddling
them again.

Smirking, Honawu turned to Father and spoke in Hopi:
'This girl is not so bad to look at. And the boy is quick on
the feet and quick in the head. A stout boy. Better let me
take him. I need a stout, smart boy. I would put something better than rags on his back, too, and good fat on
those scarecrow bones.'

Father's only reply was a grunt. Arms crossed on breast,
he leaned against his wagon-wheel and looked far off and
grunted.

Honawu spoke lower: 'There's your old debt to me, you
remember? And there are other matters lately come to our
attention ——'

Father's lids flickered.

'One has told me that certain things have vanished from
their abiding-place. It might be necessary that the clan be
told of this loss. Yet that would be an unlucky thing, for
the clan would be displeased.'

His words fell like blows on the hearts of the Family.
The loss, then, had become known. But how?

Vensi's frightened mind hunted an explanation. With
Honawu you could never tell. He might even have been
crouching at their door when Mother told Father of the
great misfortune, for it had been early when the Family
went to bed that night. He might have come to visit —
and to pry — and, hearing voices, have paused to glean
what he could. Something had wakened Vensi: perhaps it
was the sliding feet of Honawu.

Or through the priests he might have had it, for the
priests were said to see into the deepest mysteries ... Or —
could Father have carelessly told someone? ... Or Mother?
... Or Nuva?

Father was standing as still as a katchina doll. Mother,
her face gray, went on automatically hitching up one knee
and then the other to tilt the *tiposhoya's* cradle. Omva
climbed on Vensi's shoulders and tried to strangle her with
affectionate arms. Through the child's small cries and the
pounding of her own heart Vensi listened for what more
should be said.

From his pocket Honawu took a rectangle of tin, folded
like a book, and with it mechanically plucked the sparse
hairs from his chin and upper lip. 'With Nuva my son and
Vensi the daughter of my sister,' he said softly, 'our families would be as one, and all these unhappy matters could
well be hidden and forgot.'

'He covets us,' Vensi thought, as she had thought often
before; 'in spite of our being witch-children he wants us;
but more he wants to strike at Father and Mother by taking
us away.' She waited, stifling, for Father's reply.

Again there was an interruption. The Agent, Mongwi,
drove his automobile up beside the Family's team, so that
the mules skittered nervously, and the nearer one shied
against the farther. Mongwi came and laid a hand on Father's shoulder. Like other *bohannas*, he seemed to think it
needful to touch the person he spoke with.

'I've something to talk over with you,' he said.

'Now at last it has really come,' thought Vensi. 'Now he is going to say that the Family must be divided, as well as the flock.'

12. THE SMOKING CHIMNEY

NOT at once did Father tell the Family what Mongwi had talked about so long and earnestly. Not until the hoofs of the gray mules were twinkling along toward the ranch did he tell.

When she could wait no longer Mother faltered: 'Did Mongwi think our children still too thin? Did he wish to take them from us?'

'Not just now,' Father said. 'No, this time as a friend he spoke with me, telling me what we might do if we wished, to bring silver that would help us through the year.'

He waited, tantalizingly, for Mother to nudge him on. 'Silver?' she asked wonderingly.

'Yes, silver. This is the way of it: Because I weave good blankets and you *fairly* good baskets; and because, besides, the boy-baby would be a marvel to the *bohannas* who have not seen Indian albinos; and because our boy and girl and our little sister are not very bad-looking as young ones go ... for all these reasons' — he flicked the mules with the rope end of his whip and let a twinkle leak through his solemnity as he kept the Family waiting — 'for all these reasons we may if we like go to a far *bohanna* city and show the whites how our people live and work and dress. Not, of course,' he added with a laugh, looking down at his shabby jeans, 'how we dress for every day, but how we dress for the dances, in the old Hopi style.'

'Whirls Fair,' Nuva commented. 'In school we have heard all about Whirls Fair.'

'I thought the family of Lahpoo went from Oraibi,' said Mother. 'Do they want two Hopi families, then?'

'They want enough to make some of the dances,' Father answered.

'It is too far to drive the mules, I suppose?' asked Mother. 'Then where should we sleep by the way? And how take enough piki for the journey? And the goats for the boy-baby's milk, now that he is used to goat's milk?'

'Yes, certainly to drive the mules would take far too long,' Father answered seriously. 'But Mongwi says all those things would be taken care of. He says they have even built Hopi houses that we should stay in while we were there. And the money would be as much as we usually handle in many moons.'

'How much money?' Nuva asked practically.

'Enough to carry us there,' Father answered, 'and a certain amount for our food while we remain, and then, over and above, forty-five dollars for the month ... And,' he added, 'Mongwi thinks we can sell our work, also. Hundreds of *bohannas*: thousands, he says, swarming like ants over an anthill.'

Vensi felt dizzy. 'Does Mongwi say we must go?' she asked faintly.

'Mongwi says neither yes nor no. It is not his affair: he only tells us about it. Word came to him that the Whirls Fair *bohannas* were asking for such a family, and his thought turned to us. If the *tiposhoya* is now strong and grown enough so that the journey would not make a danger for him: that is the only question Mongwi asks. The matter is for us to decide.'

'And what did you answer him?' Mother inquired.

'I said we could not, anyway, go before the Niman Katchina, and after that I would let him know. He said, All right, but that the man who wrote him will not be satisfied with being put off so. *Bohannas* are always in a hurry.'

'I don't care to make a show of myself before a lot of staring whites,' Nuva said with dignity. Then his eyes brightened with a new thought: 'It wouldn't be bad to ride on one of their trains, though.'

'I have seen their trains,' said Father. 'Several of their trains.'

'Should we have to dance before the *bohannas*?' Vensi murmured in dismay.

'Still,' Mother reminded her, 'to dance for the whites would be pain that would last only a short while; and it might mean a dress and a warm jacket for school, and the shoes you are so set on.'

'Yes, and Whirls Fair will hold many wonders,' Father added.

That was true, and a part of Vensi wished to see them. On the other hand, she had heard tales of other Hopis who had gone to fairs, and the tales were alarming. Even Miss Rivers talked, talked everlastingly. 'Won't you have

more potatoes?' she had asked Vensi that day at dinner.
'Oh, do have more potatoes!' As if once asking and answering were not plenty.

Those far *bohannas* knew Indians far less than did Miss
Rivers. They thought an Indian was a wild animal or else
a god. And some of them thought he was a clown, for
giving fun and laughter by everything he did.

All these matters the Family considered. Yet much as
they discussed the question, they were careful to tell no
one else about it, even when they had gone back from the
ranch to the House on Top. And the preparations for the
Niman Katchina left small time for neighborly gossip,
if they had been tempted to tell.

In midwinter the Katchinas, the Ancient Ones, came
up from the Underworld, and the Hopis held a celebration
in honor of their coming. Now, in July, when the crops
were nearly made, the spirits went home to the depths
whence the Hopi forefathers had climbed by way of the
Grand Canyon, back in the mists of forgotten time; and in
honor of the departure the Hopis again made festival.

It kept everybody busy, preparing for the Niman, the
Homegoing. In the House on Top everyone but Omva and
the *tiposhoya* was at work; and Nuva. Nuva had all he
could do to tend the flock, with his bruised knee still stiff
and painful. Tawamana's uncle, who was the Bone Doctor,
had pulled the joint into place and promised that it would
be well in a week; and the Bone Doctor was always right;
but the week was not over and so the knee was not yet well.

Mother and Vensi ground corn and made piki and
worked at top speed weaving new basket-trays to hold both
meal and bread. Father must go at dawn each day to one
or another of his widespread fields; and now he had also
other matters, which kept him half the night away from
the House on Top.

During their earlier years, these mysterious absences

had puzzled Nuva and Vensi. Then much had been mysterious and puzzling about the Katchina dances, and it had been terrifying as well as delightful to watch the huge painted beings with their towering headdresses and their gaily embroidered kilts and sashes come dancing and shouting through the village. For were not these the very Ancients come up from below — the spirits whose bright images the children were each year given? Vensi and Nuva were seven or eight years old before they doubted the verity of the Katchinas.

Then, when they had reached the age of curiosity, and might be expected to root out the truth for themselves, the village took them into its confidence.

Vensi would not forget the day when they were led down into one of the kivas, wide-eyed and shaking and not knowing what to expect. Father and Mother had opposed their going for yet another year; that the children guessed; but the force of village opinion and village determination were too strong for Father and Mother.

Vensi and Nuva had their sponsors to cling to; but even these grown-ups could do no more than hold the children's small, chill hands and murmur encouragement. The ordeal was something every Hopi child must go through.

Above them suddenly loomed the Whipping Katchina, majestic and terrible, a bunch of yucca spines in his hand. With the yucca he flogged the boy and girl, till tongues of flame darted over their bodies, and blood oozed after flame. And while they stood shuddering with held-back sobs, it was explained to them that the Katchina dances were remembering ceremonies, attentions to please the Ancients; and that the gigantic creatures were men of the village, their own fathers and uncles and neighbors, dressed and masked to represent the Powerful Ones. And all the trembling boys and girls present were warned that they who had been given a glimpse of sacred matters must not whisper a word of the revelation to younger children, not ready for such knowledge. If they were to do so, their punishment would be bitter: they would be whipped, not with yucca, whose sharp blades left wounds that soon healed, but with cactus, whose lacerations caused death.

Whether such punishment had ever befallen anyone, Nuva and Vensi did not know; but the threat was sufficient to keep the secret from generation to generation of Hopi children. It is sufficient today.

Now, Vensi and Nuva knew even where the paraphernalia of the Katchinas was kept, in a cave above a certain perpendicular cliff under Middle Village. They knew that the men would set long ladders against that blank rock wall and clamber up them to the cave, there to dress for their visit to the village. Next year, maybe, Nuva would be joining them there, to mend and repaint masks and put costumes in order, as Father did now.

Yes, it took time, much time, to make ready for these elaborate shows and carry them out. Impossible to care as the Hopis wished for the flocks and the fields, the home and the children, while everything was being made grand for the gods. But what could be done? If the messengers of the gods did not carry home friendly words to the Underworld, the harm to flock and fields, to home and children, would be greater than any temporary neglect could cause. So said the Old Ones of the tribe.

And, besides, the ceremonies were the social events of the mesas, rich with color and excitement. The gay grotesquerie of the Katchinas wove itself through Hopi life like gaudy threads in a tapestry.

But the Niman Katchina was not all the Family was thinking about, during these blazing July days. In the back of their minds stood always the thought of Whirls Fair; and for Whirls Fair, Mongwi had explained, the finest Hopi clothes would be a necessity.

Mother, of course, had a handwoven Hopi dress, and buckskin moccasins and leg-wrappings; and so also had Vensi. Now Father set to weaving a dress for Omva. Every spare minute he used at his loom, and it was lucky that Omva was so small, for this was slow weaving, and hard by the dim light of evening, with the colors so dark.

The Family had also to go to the moccasin-maker and have Omva measured for footwear. For the rest, if they decided to go to Whirls Fair, Lomavoya would stake them for the men's shirts and trousers, and for the women's gay summer shawls. Without doubt he would also release their silver from pawn.

But as yet the elders could not make up their minds to do this thing. In every village, nowadays, there were people who had traveled afar; yet such a journey still loomed strange and fearful. It was too much like shooting oneself forth into the trackless ways of the clouds and the deep sky.

On the other hand, there was the promise of much money to pull them, and the growing unfriendliness of Honawu and Mutz and their friends to push them. That unfriendliness was like a bad smell that was seeping through the rest of the village. It would be good to get away from it; and it would be good to have enough money to pay what Honawu claimed Father owed him. Only, as Mother said, better hold fast the broken piki in your hand than drop it and reach for the rainbow.

At last, through all the working and all the wondering, came the main day of the feast, when the Katchinas danced around the villages and hooted to the children at the house doors. In the afternoon there were gifts for everyone: piki colored red with chillies, piki made from yellow corn and from blue, and a few drums and gourd-rattles and katchina dolls. There were not so many gifts and contests as at Powamu, the February festival of the arrival of the Ancients; but there were enough to make the day a gay one.

Yet for the Family it could not be wholly gay, not with its evil smell of unfriendliness. And in the evening that smell became a stench.

Katchinas were dancing and clowns were playing crude pranks and cutting capers that brought loud laughter. The 'crying-time' of day had come, when any announcements were made, the criers standing high on the housetops and calling their news, their invitations, to the people below. The shrill hoot of one of the Witch Katchina's striped clowns lifted all eyes to Mother's housetop, where he stood; and when he had everyone's attention, the clown began to call out in the chanting tone of the crier.

'Listen, you of Middle Village!' he bade them in a high falsetto. 'Old, Precious Things of the tribe, brought by us Ancients from the Underworld — these are gone from the place to which we entrusted them. Gone! Have they crept away back with our brothers, the snakes? Have they flown with the souls of the eagles? Have they starved, because she who should have fed them has been wandering after strange gods and has forgot them? Ask, but do not expect to learn.'

Hooting again, he clambered, with an odd, sidewise agility, down the two ladders. A great uproar of question followed his words, and doubtful laughter. Vensi, looking out from under the huddled folds of her shawl, thought that many of the villagers were ignorant of what or of whom the clown spoke. But there were others. There were others who kept their eyes too carefully away from Father and Mother.

When the Family was safe in the house that night, after hours when all had tried to act as if nothing disturbing had happened, Vensi murmured in a choked voice to Nuva:

'That clown — was he not of the size and of the crooked shape of Honawu?'

'I have asked myself that same question,' Nuva answered. 'And his fashion upon the ladders — sidewise ——'

Perhaps even this unpleasantness might not have decided

the elders to go to Whirls Fair, if a second and a third, yes, and a fourth, had not quickly followed.

Next morning the stove smoked heavily when Mother started the fire. In a few moments the room had grown bitter with choking fumes.

'Something must have fallen into the chimney,' Mother said, coughing and rubbing her eyes. 'Run, daughter, and clear it out.'

Vensi ran. As she went she seized Nuva's stout rabbit-stick, and laughingly evaded him when he protested and limped after her. She was up the ladder and on the roof in a minute. The chimney was at the back corner, where the house wall fell straight away to the edge of the mesa, three stories down, and the edge of the mesa to the horse corral, and the edge of the horse corral to the ledge far below.

The chimney was a low one, a stack of flawed earthenware pots turned upside down and with their bottoms broken out. Vensi poked down through them vigorously with the rabbit-stick, and felt something give and drop. Instantly the smoke rushed up. Whatever had clogged the chimney now lay on the fire below.

Satisfied, Vensi whirled about to run down again. Instead, her feet shot out from under her and she was hanging from the outer corner of the roof, her feet kicking the stones in vain search for a foothold. The fingers of one hand were dragging painfully across the rough adobe, the other still grasping the rabbit-stick.

'Brother! Father!' she called, breathlessly; but she knew they could not reach her in time, Father slowed by the years, Nuva by his stiffened knee.

She had a swift picture of herself dropping through the thin blue air and bouncing to the ledge where the horses would be milling with frantic hoofs and teeth. Even as she pictured the fall, her one hand was dragged from the adobe by the weight of her body. At the same instant the other hand was stopped with a wrenching jerk.

Dizzily she realized what had happened: the sturdy oak boomerang had broken through the adobe and come up against a roof-pole, and its slight curve was helping to hold it there. If she could cling to the end of the stick, with her arm pulling out of the shoulder-socket, cling till those climbing feet could gain the roof ——

The heavy wire with which the boomerang had been mended helped and harmed at once: it gave a firmer grip even while its end tore into her flesh.

Another moment and Father was drawing her up over the edge to safety.

To Mother he said: 'There was grease. Grease on the roof.'

'Oh, no,' she protested.

'Oh, yes,' he insisted. 'Well you know that Hopis do not fall from housetops, bred up as they are like flies to walk on the ceilings. Not when they are neither sick nor blind nor lame.'

'They — whoever it was — thought it would be you or I who would climb up to clear that chimney they had clogged, maybeso,' Mother said, suddenly surrendering.

And that night Father came home from his fields, long after dusk, his face dark and set. Burros had been led into his acre of early corn, he told the Family, and into his bean patch. They had trampled and eaten until half the crops were ruined.

'Led?' Mother cried in shocked unbelief. 'Surely not led?'

'Led. Carefully I looked, and I found a moccasin track; not mine, since both my moccasins are patched . . . They think to show that the gods are punishing us. But why their hate should burn so continually hotter and faster, that I cannot explain.'

With all the worry and excitement, it was not strange, perhaps, that Mother fell sick that night. Thus, Vensi

knew, any one of the Mission-Marys would have explained
the event; but Vensi had her own opinion. The pains
through Mother's head; the pains through her stomach;
were not these precisely the sort of pains the Witch Clan
would have chosen to send her? And Honawu's clan, was it
not allied to the Witch Clan?

So she thought as she silently brewed Mother a draft of
the sage tea which sometimes helped; and the thought was
speedily made certain in her mind. For as close and clear as
if the creature were perched upon the chimneypots, the yowl
and screech of a cat sounded through the House on Top.

Nuva wanted to chase the witch; for if you caught one
and exposed it for what it was — an ill-wishing Hopi of
the Witch Clan — then within a short while that Hopi

would die and his persecutions be ended. But Father said,
No; and grimly he mounted the ladder to the roof himself.

Presently he came back breathing gustily. Their ques-
tioning eyes he answered with a shake of the head.

'Over to Lenmana's roof it leaped and was gone,' he said,
when he had caught his breath. 'By the time I got to the
street there was nothing of it anywhere ... It looked,' he
added grudgingly, 'like Lenmana's gray tomcat, the one
with the torn ear.'

But of course, Vensi thought, stroking back Mother's
hair from her brow, it would look like what it wanted to
look like. A member of the Witch Clan could change into
a cat as easily as he could change his shirt.

'Let us go away!' groaned Mother, clutching at her pain.
'Let us go to Whirls Fair. It cannot be worse than this.
And at least we should have peace a little while.'

'*Antsa*,' Father agreed, 'verily.'

13.   'ARE THERE ALWAYS THIS MANY PEOPLE?'

EXCEPT for the ceremonies, bound as they are by the rhythmic movements of the sun, time is not a Big Chief in Hopi land. Occasionally Vensi brought a calendar home from school; but when vacation came, the Family forgot calendars. And the House on Top had never yet heard the tick of a clock.

Now, however, time took command. That very evening Father trudged down, quietly, to the Mission-Mary's, and telephoned to Mongwi; and Nuva went to Shungopavy,

to the moccasin-maker, to hurry him with the small moccasins, the white leg-wrappings, for Omva.

Father had used the telephone before, but not so often
but that he felt foolish, shouting into a box on the wall.
He said he felt so foolish that he could not make out what
Mongwi was saying when finally he got the Chief. The
desert telephones, besides, were hard to use: they were half
the time out of repair.

Miss McClung finally took pity on Father and listened
and talked for him, and thus he made known his decision.
His confusion clearing, he could hear the impatient rattle
and bark of the small man's reply at Miss McClung's ear:
Mongwi was saying he guessed the World's Fair man would
be all in a lather. Mongwi said also that the Agency truck
was going to the Railroad in two days, and could the Family
be ready so soon as that?

Father thought about the greased roof and the ruined
fields and the witch-cat, and moistened his lips with his
tongue and answered that they could, though two suns
was not long enough for all they must do.

Mongwi said he would try to get a wire through to
World's Fair, and he banged the receiver back into its
hook before Father could tell Miss McClung the next thing
he wanted to say. So she wound four shorts with the crank
that stuck out on the side of the telephone box, and listened,
and rang again, with a rapidity and energy that made
Father feel as slow as a turtle and as jittery as a rabbit's
nose.

What Father wanted to ask was, Could the truck pick
up the Family at First Mesa instead of at home? The
Family must go to First Mesa anyway, and if they were to
load their equipment in the Agency truck in the sight of
all Middle Village — Father did not know how Honawu
could stop them, but he felt sure Honawu would try.

Thus it was arranged. The husband of Father's sister

agreed to take Father's flock, together with his own, and to watch the Family fields. He himself had many sheep but few acres to tend, so he could easily manage.

There were now no Old, Precious Things to be served; their care need not be provided for. As for the peaches and what was left of the early corn, the Family would be back soon enough for the harvest. The apricots were already ripe, and the Family picked what they could and left the rest for Aunt's household.

Her boy drove the six to First Mesa on the day before Mongwi's truck was due. All afternoon and evening they spent at the trading-post, fitting themselves out for their adventure. Fortunately Lomavoya had sateen shirts, ready-made, which suited Father and Nuva well enough. Father chose black, piped at shoulders, collar, and cuffs with white, and Nuva took orange, piped with black. Lomavoya sold them silver shells for buttons down the front, and returned them from pawn Nuva's ring and bow-guard and their belts. Father's belt was set with silver *conchos* as big as saucers, and Nuva's, a good eight inches wide, was patterned with bright steel disks. Father picked out a scarlet silk handkerchief to tie around his head and Nuva a green one. Moccasins and plain trousers completed their outfits.

Mother's jewelry and Vensi's came out of pawn, too, and gave their necks and wrists and fingers self-respect. And the whole Family bent over the tray of baby jewelry for a half-hour, selecting a bracelet to buy with Omva's fifty-cent prize. It had no turquoise, but instead a Zuni raindrop design, big and bright, in its center.

Then the women chose summer shawls from the long line pinned by their corners to a rope: Vensi a white cashmere with many-colored flowers, Mother a black one with red roses, and Omva a little scarlet one with flowers like Vensi's.

All these purchases Lomavoya's clerk wrote down, for,

rich and powerful as the trader was, and with a fine car
and a fine house, he had never learned to read and write.

The Family spent that night with clan-relations on
First Mesa. It was easy for unexpected guests to be taken
care of, even six at a time, when they need only roll themselves up on the sheepskins to sleep, and when the dining-
table could be extended without turning a hair, the size
of the floor its only limit.

'When I was young,' Mother said, 'I should have been
wild with excitement: it was so seldom that we visited
another mesa.'

Yes, and even now such visiting was rare enough to
excite Nuva and Vensi. It was only the coming journey,
stretching miles without number, that made this one seem
small and tame.

Next day the Agency truck, with its Hopi driver, chugged
up the mesa road and across the narrow causeway of rock
that separated the two front villages. The Family needed
a truck, for their bedding must go, and the loom and bat-
tens and spindle and cards and wool; and the women's
basket-stuffs; and a store of piki and apricots and beans
and corn meal and canned milk and Karo and corn to
make hominy. The mutton, Miss McClung had said, they
could buy at Whirls Fair.

All was hurry and confusion. The men crammed things
tightly into the truck, moving them in and out and making
a great and satisfied to-do about their being so well packed,
as if no one had ever packed so skilfully before.

'But that bag of piki?' Mother inquired.

'The piki is in,' Father assured her.

'But where?' Mother persisted, poking here and there
amid the mass.

Vensi found it at last, stowed under the loom-poles,
where it would have been ground to bits before it reached
even the Railroad. They were sure no Hopi could live

without piki; so they unloaded their end of the truck and
repacked with the piki on top. Then Mother climbed in
and sat on the flour bag of baby clothes, and Vensi handed
up the *tiposhoya* in his cradle, and retrieved Omva from a
neighboring piki room where she had got her face and hands
and clean dress black with soot from the chimney.

Flushed with excitement, Nuva and Vensi got in beside
Mother, and Father beside the driver, and they went jolting down the looped mesa road.

'We are late,' the driver said, squinting at the sun.
'We must drive fast if we are to get the tickets before
your train comes.'

'Maybe you will take that short road across below
Second Mesa,' Father suggested hopefully.

'It is so rough we should lose more time than we could
gain.'

Father squared his shoulders resignedly against the
seat-cushion. He had hoped that they would not take the
road that ran along the side of the mesa, below Middle
Village. Through the school grounds went that road,
where Honawu was likely to be working, doing carpentry
for the new laundry building ... Yes, it was hard to say
how Honawu could possibly stop them from going to
Whirls Fair; but Honawu was ingenious.

And Honawu was nearer at hand than Father guessed.
As the truck swung past the side of the trading-post and
turned on the Second Mesa road, a crooked small figure
burst out of the trading-post doorway, and Honawu stood
there, waving his arms and shouting.

'You wish to stop for this man?' the driver asked, with
an amused side-glance at Father. 'Honawu, of your village,
isn't it?'

Father shook a fervent head. 'No time to stop,' he said.

A moment Honawu stood as if baffled on the high stone
steps, and then he scrambled down them and ran up the

hill behind the store where his hobbled horse was grazing. Vensi and Nuva watched open-mouthed, and Father murmured to the driver, 'This wagon can't, I suppose, go any faster?'

'Faster than the Wash when it is up,' the driver bragged, and stepped on the gas. 'You would like it better not to see our friend Honawu, maybeso,' he added, grinning.

Father grunted a heartfelt affirmative.

By the time Honawu had unhobbled his horse and mounted it and was galloping along the road, the truck had a mile's headway; and the mile lengthened fast. Vensi giggled behind her hands, and Nuva leaned over the tailboard, watching with eyes that laughed. Father sat tight, his neck cords stiff. Now Honawu's sorrel was lost in a hollow, now it was a silhouette on a hilltop; but steadily it grew smaller, and after a while it was lost to sight.

Swiftly the truck ate up the miles between First Mesa and Second Mesa, plowing through the sand beside the windmill, whizzing past the small community around church and Mission, climbing up among the tumbled hills to the side of the mesa, past Lemova Spring, past Corn Rock, to the cottonwood green and the tamarisk gray of the school grounds ... No Honawu to fear here now ... Down the hill and onto the plain again, where the truck really picked up speed.

Eighty miles or so, measured the road to the Railroad, and Vensi had not dreamed eighty miles could be so quickly swallowed. Over drifted sand, across shuddering rock, nosing down into little washes and rearing up out of them, the truck rattled and swayed at fifty miles an hour.

Mother clutched the baby-basket close and bowed her head above it so that she need not see how fast the desert streaked by. Omva, who had fallen asleep, woke and blinked astonished, sleep-swollen eyes. Father folded his arms across his chest and acted as if he didn't notice the speed, though the big blue triangles of turquoise jumped and danced in his ears.

As for Nuva and Vensi, they got the giggles; and what with laughing so hard and jolting so hard, Vensi felt like the gelatine dessert the school cook sometimes served them at noon: quivering from center to circumference.

For two hours they raced on, flying past the Giant's Chair, vast shape of stone sitting alone among its rattlesnakes; past other buttes, which the children and Mother had never before seen except as small shapes afar off. There was the one that the Navajos called Tees Toh, and the one shaped like the chocolate candies at the trading-post, and Chimney Butte.

What was most interesting was to see the other side of them. It was like seeing the other side of pictures on a wall, and finding the back entirely different from the front. Chimney Butte, for instance, had always resembled a chimney of rounded Hopi pots, stacked upside down. Now, behold, it was like the Capitol of the United States: a picture of the Capitol hung in one of the rooms at school.

They passed two trading-posts, crouching solitary in the desert. They passed a few Navajo hogans and a few flocks of sheep and goats with silent boy or girl herders who revolved to watch their going. They passed the edge of the Painted Desert, with its gullied-out bowl shapes many-colored.

And then they came to the real wonder: the town.

The young people, and Mother, too, would have liked to ride up one street and down another, looking at the houses of *bohannas* and Mexicans; watching the clusters of *bohannas* and Mexicans, Hopis and Navajos, clogging the doorways of the stores. But with all their speed it was nearly train time, and the tickets were yet to buy. The driver, who had bought tickets before, helped them with that transaction; and, anyway, one of Mongwi's wires had given the ticket agent instructions.

Then came the train. The Family stood still in a long
line, and with calm faces watched the monster steam and
snort and clang up to the front of the station. They looked
as if they had seen a few assorted trains every day of their
lives, and were pretty badly bored by this one.

The truth was that Vensi's heart, at least, jumped within
her, fluttering in her throat and mixing itself with her
breath. She was not exactly afraid, for she knew that this
too was ordinary *bohanna* magic. But the huge size of the
thing, its black bulk, its roar, the fury with which its steel
arms hurled its wheels around, all together made it hard
to stand perfectly still and let it charge toward her with
only a foot or two to spare. Even when it stopped, its
white breath blew out with a furious hissing, so close that
it nearly touched her.

But harder for Vensi than this ordeal was that of following Mother and climbing aboard, where close-packed ranks
of whites stared up at her from their seats as the Family
filed through one long coach and another and another.
The driver led the way, his jauntiness drawing into its shell
as he went. Still, he knowingly manipulated the divided
seats when he reached some empty ones, so that four were
facing each other. And he plumped the hand luggage down
on one just opposite, where he motioned Nuva to sit.
Even though he fell silent before the *bohannas*, he had
made good his boast of train wisdom. The Family was
sorry to see him go, when the mystic cry, 'Allllll Aboarrrrd!'
rang out, snapping up at the end with triumphant finality.

The Family had never known days and nights so bewildering as those that followed. Before the first afternoon
had passed, Mother was tired and numb with dangling her
short legs from the seat, she who was used to nothing but
folding them comfortably on the floor. Nor could she
learn the trick of walking up the aisle when the train was
moving; always she went lurching against people's annoyed

shoulders, or she grasped desperately at their newspapers, or — once — staggered full into a *bohanna* lap.

Sometimes it was Father who led Omva up and down when she grew restless, but oftener the task fell to Vensi, and to her it was torture. Omva found endless fun in the dangerous promenades, in the pointed paper cups of ice water, in having her hands washed with meal-like soap in the shiny metal lavatory. The only way Vensi could live through the stares and questions of the passengers was to pretend she was blind and deaf, and go lurching along, wholly intent on Omva, until she could escape to her seat next the window and shut herself away by fixing her gaze on the flying world outside.

New and strange were even the commonest details of life, like eating and sleeping. For food the Family had their sacks of piki and apricots, but they had besides bewildering *bohanna* meals. At first Father shook his head when the friendly waiter made him understand that a dinner could be brought to them in the coach.

'All paid for, boss,' the waiter finally told Father. 'Better you git while the gittin's good.'

Father agreed.

Finding Nuva the spokesman for the party, the waiter then showed him the bill of fare, and tactfully read the items aloud as his big brown finger pointed them out.

'You all like roas' loin of pork?' he asked, 'Or —— '

'Yess,' Nuva replied with dignity.

'Or chicken-fry steak —— '

'Yess,' said Nuva.

'Or here's Virginia baked ham, mighty good —— '

'Yess,' Nuva answered.

'Or hamburger with onions —— '

'Yess.'

'And halibut steak — that's fish —— '

'Yess.'

The waiter rolled his eyes perplexedly. 'Well, which, young boss?' he inquired.

'A some of all,' said Nuva.

Breathing heavily, the waiter at length departed. He returned with a table which he set between their knees; and, again, with trays on which dishes were stacked three deep. The Family accepted them as if such floods of food were commonplace.

So also did Father and Mother accept the table, though it was the first time they had ever eaten at one. With complete poise they tried even the most unfamiliar and repellent of the foods. But they could make small headway against the abundance, and the waiter did some more heavy breathing when he had to carry half of it back to the kitchen.

Dessert was more successful, for it was ice cream. Omva was the only member of the Family to whom ice cream was a complete novelty. At the first taste she opened her mouth and let the cream slide out on her chin. 'Hot!' she gasped, with amazed eyes on Vensi, who had given it to her. But almost at once the sweetness and flavor parted her lips for another bite, which she worked around in her mouth with a gingerly tongue, eyes still startled.

After that first meal the waiter did not show the Family a bill of fare. He brought them what he thought they should like.

He even inquired anxiously about the *tiposhoya's* bottle, being both fascinated and astonished at this 'towhaid papoose.'

'I cain't figure how you keep his milk sweet,' he said, shaking his head. 'Now, my young ones, seems like they always have to have their milk just so or they up and get sick on us. Looks to me like you better give me the rest of them bottles to put in the re-frigerator, if you don't want to have trouble.'

This was what the Mission-Mary had advised: that they have a porter put the bottles in the icebox; but it had been too complicated a business for the Family to cope with.

It was the waiter, too, who suggested, when night came, that they boost the cradle up on the baggage rack, where it fitted securely. The vibration of the train and the flow of fresh air together worked like a charm, and the boy-baby slept with few wakings.

It was fortunate that he did, for night was difficult. As the train grew more and more crowded, the whole Family was jammed into the two double seats, with their luggage piled around them. They dovetailed together as best they could, the chair-backs lowered and the center arms let down. Omva stretched out across two laps and apparently noticed little change from the home sheepskin. But the others were bothered by the lights, even when they were dimmed, and by the crowds. Vensi would slip off to sleep, only to awaken sick at her stomach with shock as passengers surged past her in the aisle, getting off or getting on; or when the steady motion of the train gave place to sudden stillness; or when the lights of a station flared in her face or another train rocketed past. Young as she was, her back felt as if it were broken in two, and she pitied Mother, who doubtless ached much harder, being so very old.

The daytime was better, with fresh marvels to see: villages and new kinds of farms rushing headlong past their windows; cities thick with smoke, vast rivers, trees such as she had not supposed existed in the whole world.

Before the two days had passed, the Family felt themselves old inhabitants of the glass village that roared through the countryside: so many of the other passengers had got off since they got on, so many new ones had taken the places of the departed. Vensi began to dread leaving the train for the city to which it was taking them.

The hour for arrival came.   The conductor — who
treated the Family like bad children when he was in a
hurry and like good children when he was not — ordered
them to get their things together and be ready.   They piled
their luggage on the seats and waited while the train drew
into the railroad yards; stood in the aisle in the long line
of outgoing passengers, swaying forward all together, and
jerking back as the train jolted.   And finally they stumbled
down by the portable step.   Then they stood petrified with
uncertainty in the clangor.

Someone was supposed to meet them, but no one met them. They stood in a close huddle, looking proud and aloof, while hundreds of whites hurtled past them, whirled around them, pushed against them. Vensi remembered what Father had once said, that the *bohannas* were as the waters of Oraibi Wash when it was high, each drop a man. His saying was true, and here the Family stood in the midst of the Wash, as helpless inside as they were indifferent outside.

Mother spoke without moving her head. 'Are there always this many people?' she asked unbelievingly.

THEIR colored waiter rescued them from the whirlpool.

'Didn't nobody meet you, boss?' he asked genially. 'Well, we fix that all right.'

He called another dark brown man, this one in a blue shirt instead of a white jacket, and with red-crowned cap atilt. 'You be a Boy Scout now,' the waiter adjured him; and to the Family he said: 'This boy, he'll take good care of you. Good-bye, folks. Have a good time and look out you don't scalp nobody.' He flashed a white smile at them and waved his hand.

The words set the Family in motion, and they followed the redcap, Father carrying Omva and Mother lugging the cradle. A lusty roar came from beneath the swathing blankets. The *tiposhoya* did not approve of this air, hot and thick with tobacco and people and coal-dust.

The station which they entered was not a building at all, Vensi thought: for who could conceive of stones and mortar holding together in tiers as tall as a mesa? No, it was a world, and its vaulted ceiling was a sky turned to glass and metal, with people small as ants swarming beneath it, as Mongwi had said, and endless stairs leading up and leading down, and chanting voices echoing back from that frozen zenith.

The redcap brought them to a counter behind which sat women. Above the women hung a sign, and Nuva and Vensi spelled out its words: 'Trav-el-ers' Aid.' The words did not help them: 'aid'; what was 'aid'?

Mongwi had sent Father a letter for use if he got into difficulties. This seemed the time to use it, and Father unpinned it from the breast pocket of his shirt and handed it to one of the women. She read it, nodded, looked at the Family, and said, Yes, she understood, and she would telephone, and they were to wait. She telephoned, and they waited, sitting stolidly on one of the nearest long seats.

'That Wiki,' said Nuva, speaking straight ahead of him, 'he has certainly never seen anything to equal this. To Phoenix he has been, and to Prescott, but I suppose you could put the whole of Phoenix and Prescott into this one house.'

'Honawu's girl, too,' Vensi contributed. 'She talks so much about Santa Fe and how big the school was there... But all the same I would be glad to be back where she is and let her come here.' For here the noises seemed to crash around Vensi's head like stones falling from the mesa.

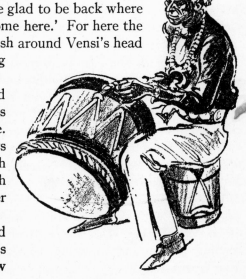

'Well, yes,' said Nuva, 'but yet it is something to see. They have always said there were such people and such houses, but I never believed it.'

With fascinated horror Vensi was watching a new

throng of travelers pouring endlessly down a broad stair.
'I believed it,' she said, 'like when they tell about the
Underworld and how our grandfathers climbed up out of
there. I believed it — but I didn't suppose it was really so.'

In a short while another man, in another kind of cap,
came after the Family. This man took some pasteboards
Father had been keeping, and carried them to a grated
window and left them there.

'Taxi's outside,' he said, jerking his thumb; and he
tramped away.

The Family trudged after him, Mother scurrying and
murmuring breathlessly to Father about the loom and
the bedding and the other things. When they had woven
in and out through the crowd outside the station to the
bright yellow automobile where the man waited, Nuva
asked about that baggage. It was all right, the man said:
that was what the pasteboards were about; no, the loom
and bedding weren't lost; they would come soon, in another
automobile. Mother was all for waiting and making sure;
but the man held open the door of the yellow automobile
and forced her to get in by staring over her head.

The taxicab dashed through traffic like a racing horse.
It was reined back on its heels at corners, and it shot forward, Vensi soon saw, whenever the rest of the herd shot
forward, though it was usually one jump ahead of them.
Nuva grunted and pointed with his chin, and then she saw
that the herd stopped when a red light flashed on in the
middle of the road, and that it started again when the
red light exchanged itself for green and a man in white
blew a shrill whistle and turned his edge toward the herd.

Vensi gripped the seat with one hand and held tight to
Omva with the other, lest the child be jarred loose when
the taxi jerked to a stop. Again they were in Oraibi Wash,
but now each drop was not a *bohanna* man but a *bohanna*
automobile. Vensi stole a glance at Mother: her eyes were

shut, and she clasped the cradle close beneath her shawl.
Omva was silent but delighted, and Nuva was grinning.
Father's face was a mask, but, feeling her eyes upon him,
he said stoutly:

'This is like the walls of the Canyon de Chelly, only in
place of rock made by the gods here are mountains made
by men. And the echo at the railway station, that was
no more than the talk-back-voice at the Canyon de Chelly,
either.'

Father's comparison was somehow comforting. Canyon
de Chelly had belonged to the Indians back to time's beginning. Before the old *bohanna* Kit Carson had rounded
up eight thousand Navajos there, and subdued them; before the Navajos first moved into the miles of fertile flats
set deep within the narrow gash; even then, the grandfathers of the Hopis had hung their huge apartment houses
in the cleft.

No, the *bohannas* hadn't so much to brag about, in these
man-made canyons of theirs that were no grander than
Canyon de Chelly.

On and on the cab darted and stopped, darted and
stopped, until at last it came to Whirls Fair. Here were
bright colored buildings, shading out like rainbows, and
water springing high in air, and great images.

'And this,' said Father, 'is like Blue Canyon.'

Vensi herself had seen Blue Canyon, out Tuba City way.
In it were crowds of white stone figures like dancing giants
frozen while they danced; and walls striped with blue and
with red; and others like the flounced skirts of Navajo
women, even to the tape sewed around their vast ruffles.
It comforted Vensi still more to think of Blue Canyon.

The next thing to give the Family courage was the
place where the driver emptied them out: a Hopi house,
sitting there between a Navajo hogan and a plains tepee.
The Hopi house had a dome-shaped oven outside it, and

steps as well as ladder leading up to its second story. And
on the ground before it sat Lahpoo and his wife Kaemana,
from Oraibi, and their three children, and their old grandfather, eating their supper as if they were on the mesa
at home.

Mother slid the baby-basket to the ground and held
Kaemana's hand long in hers, while Father clasped Lahpoo's
and the grandfather's, and the younger generation grinned
at each other. The two families had had only passing acquaintance, but now, with their twelve Hopi souls coming
together among the strange millions, acquaintance ripened
to something deep as kinship. It was like coming home,
to sit down beside these folks and eat mutton and beans
and coffee with them. For an hour they all talked steadily,
almost forgetting the outlandish crowds. But when the
Family's loom and bedding and other baggage came, and
were carried up the steps and dumped into the second story,
which was to be their place, a sudden strong weariness
gripped them, and they wanted nothing but to go to sleep.

As soon as darkness came, they rolled up on the floor.
Then long sighs of relief sounded from the bundles of
Father and Mother, it was so good to be stretched out once
more on the proper kind of bed.

It was hot — hot with all the windows open wide. It
was noisy, shrieks and honking horns and shoutings and
rumblings and roarings surrounding the small oasis of their
house. The *tiposhoya*, tired of all the changes, fretted inter-
mittently, the whole night through. And yet the Family
slept.

Once or twice Vensi woke, and leaned up on her elbow
to look out at the dazzle of lights, and at the colored flames
that shot up into the sky and curled down again. She
could see a vast wheel swinging up and over and down, and
other wheels that circled parallel with the earth, carrying
people astride animal images amid a great clangor of

music. Her breath caught with frightened wonder and
pleasure. This, she thought, was the best way to see
Whirls Fair.

As they ate breakfast next morning Mother said flatly,
but with a wryly humorous twist of the face: 'I will stay
here where I am. Always. Not for anything in the world
will I rush again through the land in a glass village that
howls like a wolf and brays like a burro.'

'Even these rich and crazy *bohannas* would not pay us
forty-five dollars a month to stay here forever, I suppose,'
said Father.

'And how are we to earn all that money?' Nuva asked,
as he had asked before.

The Family soon learned. They were to live and work
in the sight of the crowd. Before they had finished eating,
the first of the *bohannas* climbed steps and ladders to watch
them, so that their talk died, and their hands became
wooden hands, and poorly jointed, when they carried
their food to their mouths.

The whites were interested in everything. Every time
the *tiposhoya* was fed or bathed, someone was there to
watch. That he was an albino, few of them would believe.

'You say he's a full-blood Injun?' a fat red man demanded, leveling a pudgy forefinger at the *tiposhoya's*
fair loveliness. 'Go on with you! If he ain't a Swede baby
I'll eat my hat.' And he puffed down the steps, snorting
with indignation.

On the other hand, there was one serious, spectacled
man who was both delighted and excited to find the boy-
baby. He was first interested in the Family for another
reason: the designs Nuva was painting on the wall. With
Lahpoo's katchina paints Nuva was putting on, out of
his memory, ancient Hopi birds and butterflies, and patterns of sun and clouds and rain. Deep in his mind Nuva
had long thought that he could maybeso earn good money

by making these designs on walls, such as the walls of Harvey Houses or Government buildings and schools; and when he had made money he could buy paints and paper and brushes, all he wanted.

'Hopis?' the spectacled man said to Nuva, partly asking but mostly saying, and pronouncing the name for a wonder as it should be pronounced: Hope-ee.

'Yess,' Nuva assented, sweeping in a beautiful curve of butterfly wing.

The man unfolded a newspaper and peered at it through his thick glasses. 'Here,' he said, handing it to Nuva with his finger on an item. 'Taos. Related to your tribe, I believe.'

Nuva read the paragraph slowly. 'Umm,' he said, and read it again.

'Something?' Father asked.

Nuva read aloud: 'Pueblo — Indian boy — seventeen — years — wins — thousand — dollar — prize. . . . Taos boy — takes first — a-ward in — Nat-ion-al — Youth — Contest. . . . May have to hand — over prize to — Pueblo Council — ac-cording — to custom. Wants to — study art.'

Nuva handed back the paper. There was no change in the boy's expression; only an enrichment of his dark brown skin as the blood coursed fast through all his veins.

None of the Family made comment; they only became more deeply quiet in sympathy.

For this was Nuva's contest, the contest to which his schoolteacher had sent his painting of the sacred plants against a background of blue sky and ivory pueblo.

All their faces lightened, though no outsider would have noticed the lightening, when Nuva spoke.

'An Indian boy won the very great prize,' he said slowly: 'an Indian boy. Next time, maybe, it will be I — if only I can get the thick good paper and the right kind of paint.'

'And if there are more such contests,' Father warned
him.

The Family had been talking in Hopi; but the spectacled
man was no longer interested, anyway, in the subject of
Indian art. He had nodded approvingly at Nuva's wall
drawings, and made as if to commend them; and then his
attention had been drawn past them to the boy-baby and
had clung there.

Busily then he asked questions and busily he made notes
in a pocket notebook. 'Are there any other albinos among
your relations?' he asked.

'No, not any,' Nuva answered.

'Do you know of any ancestors of yours who were
albinos?'

'No,' said Nuva, 'I don' know of none.'

The questions went on and on. Were Father and Mother
cousins? Or any other relation? No, they were no relations
at all. The man wrote down all the answers, and then tried
with his watch to see whether the boy-baby could hear
well; because, he explained, scientists had a belief that all
albinos were deaf, either wholly or in part.

There was no way to get the boy-baby to tell whether
he could hear the tick of the watch or not; and though he
jumped violently when Nuva shouted at him, the scientist
said that did not prove anything, because the vibration
would have startled him, even without his hearing the
sound. So, after a long while, he went away. But first
he took Father's name and address, and said that in a year
or two he would come and visit them and ask questions
when the boy-baby could help answer them; because it
was so strange that there should have been no other albinos
and no close intermarriage in the Family. It was contrary
to all the findings of science, he said excitedly.

They all sat staring at the boy-baby when the man had
gone; and Vensi asked suddenly, 'Do you suppose the

bohanna understood that the *tiposhoya* is not our own
baby?'

But Father said he could not see what difference it made;
nor why even a pleasant man with spectacles should need
to pry into such personal affairs. The *bohannas* were too
prying, anyway; too sure of themselves.

At least ten times a day a *bohanna*, sometimes man,
sometimes woman, wanted Mother to sling the basket-
cradle from her shoulders, so that he or she could take a
picture so. Mother would not.

'She not knowing how,' Nuva finally told one of the
most persistent. 'Hopi women not doing like that. Never
carrying the *tiposie* cradle on back; only the child when
bigger.'

'Do you think we're that dumb?' cried this *bohanna*,
shiny with waved hair and strings of pearls. 'We've seen
too many pictures — photographs, too — of the squaws
carrying their papoose-cradles on their backs.'

'Not Hopis,' Nuva said stolidly. 'Squaws, maybeso,
but not Hopi ladies.'

'Hop-eyes,' most of the *bohannas* mispronounced the
tribal name; and they argued with the Indians about that
and about a great many other things. The waved ones with
pearls oftenest told how it was in the movies, and the ones
with spectacles oftenest told how it was in books. There
were so many of them who knew more about 'Hop-eyes'
than the Family had ever dreamed of, that the poor Family
grew badly confused.

At first Vensi stood with her back to the strangers, or
drew her shawl up around her mouth. But there was no
getting rid of them, so after a while she settled down beside
Mother and started an eagle basket. With her eyes fixed
on her weaving she could pretend that the whites were not
there, and that their chatter was only a radio.

Father hung his loom and began a new blanket, and

Nuva took out his Hopi top — a mere section of *bohanna* broomstick bluntly sharpened like a big pencil — and spun it with a rag tied to a stick. Omva climbed over and around her father and mother and sister, too frightened and too much interested to fret and tease.

This was the first time Omva had been dressed in proper Hopi garb, and she was so cunning that even her own people admired her with much chuckling. The whites were always trying to pick her up, when they had inspected her, often with strangely dilated nostrils, and found her clean; but Omva retreated hastily. One young girl who had courted her without success went away, only to return after a few minutes, holding out a doll.

It was a doll with shining black bangs like Omva's, and shining black eyes tilted like the baby girl's. But here the likeness stopped, for the doll was dressed in a long slim costume of flowered silk, with a broad sash tied around the middle and fashioned into a big bow behind; her sleeves were so long that they hid her tiny hands; and instead of moccasins she wore thick-soled cloth sandals.

Father twisted around from his weaving to see, and Mother paused and clucked as the girl held the doll toward Omva. Omva surveyed it unblinkingly over Vensi's shoulder.

'Not — Hopi,' said Father, puzzled. '*Bohanna*? 'Merican?'

'No,' the girl answered, 'Japanese. But doesn't it look like a twin sister of your baby?'

For a long minute Omva would make no move toward it. She thrust a fortifying thumb into her mouth instead, and let her long lashes lie on her brown cheeks. Then, as the doll came nearer and nearer, she reached out a hand, drew it back, stretched it out again, and seized the treasure.

When she had examined the doll's hair and eyes and feet and hands, its kimono and its underpinnings, she backed up to Mother with the small demanding grunts she used when her vocabulary failed her, and pulled one of Mother's hands around to her own back. Laughing, Mother took down from the wall the little red cashmere shawl, and bound the doll to Omva's back, where the tiny black bobbed head looked over the child's shoulder like a miniature of herself.

At odd moments, that first day, the two Hopi families conferred about the dance which should be given in the evening. It should be a piece of the Flute Dance, they decided, which took in maidens and little children; a piece that would not be too sacred to display here, far from its proper place and before irreverent eyes.

The *bohannas* were certainly irreverent. In the most solemn places, that night, they clapped and shouted, and some of them laughed until they cried: in the parts where most earnestly the Flute people of past ages came and begged the Snake people to let them live on the Snake mesa.

Lahpoo's old father beat the big Hopi drum for the dancing, and a resplendent figure he was, in a blue velveteen shirt and white trousers, and an abundance of silver and turquoise and shell. Rattles clattered and moccasins thudded and fox-tails twitched, all in perfect time; but it was Omva, getting underfoot and staring at the crowd, Omva in all her baby finery, that the *bohannas* seemed to like best of all.

The black wool tunic, laced over one shoulder with red yarn and leaving the other bare; the tiny squaw belt wrapped three times around her waist; the small moccasins made even smaller by the bulk of the white strips wound around her little legs; all these topped by her straight-cut mop of black hair and her wide-lashed eyes, made her a Hopi doll, and enchanting.

In those handwoven tunics, heavy as men's winter over-

coats, the women's bodies had dripped and stung with
sweat, that first day. They had not felt like cooking much
food, in the sweltering heat, and with the only cooking-
place in their second-story room a corner fireplace that
filled the house with smoke. That night the man who
seemed to own the Indians came to the Family and asked
them to cook their meals outdoors in the future, where the
people could see them do it.

It was the kind of asking, said Vensi, to which you do
not say no. In the same way the white man asked the
Family to buy bottled milk every day for babies and
young people. That would have been all right if the price
had not been so unthinkably high: twelve cents a quart —
twelve!

Next day dawned chilly and damp. It was good weather
for Hopi dresses, but for cooking outdoors it was not so
pleasant. But Mother rigged up a place for her piki griddle,
a big flat stone, black and polished, and precious because a
good piki stone is long to make. There in the sight of the
white people she knelt and made the paper bread.

Some of the *bohannas* reached over and touched the
griddle, and then exclaimed over their blistered fingers and
Mother's unscorched palm, which had firmly swept the
hot surface again and again. Most of them laughed at the
tissue-thin gray-blue bread, the good bread. Some offered
Mother coins and took bundles in exchange.

One said, 'That smoking-hot stone should certainly
sterilize it,' and set her teeth in the tissue of corn, her
companion watching her as if she were a reckless woman.

'Stare-real-ize . . . Stare-real-ize' — Vensi tried to remember the word, so that she could ask Nuva whether he
had ever met it in school. The sound of it, and the woman's
tone, and the laughter, made the blood surge hotly to
Vensi's face. She bent closer over her weaving: the eagle,
with his wings and tail-feathers spread beautifully wide,

and difficult to work. She thought: I would not stay in this place with these white people making fun of all we do and wear and eat. I would not stay, even if the mesas were fifty suns away instead of two.

WHIRLS FAIR was certainly not all bad. It held interest and enjoyment, though for days Vensi could not find them through the whirling of her thoughts, the blurring of her eyes, the roaring of her ears.

By the end of the second week she was able to forget the *bohanna* throngs enough to watch the other Hopi family at work in the dooryard.

There Lahpoo spent hours carving katchina dolls and painting them, while Kaemana made pottery. Kaemana's home was at Oraibi, Third Mesa, and only First Mesa made pottery. But Kaemana had been a First Mesa girl, and she was skilful in all the branches of the art, the tempering of the clay, the building and thinning, the polishing and painting and firing. Watching her, Vensi grew so absorbed

that she forgot herself, standing for everyone to see in the
dressed-up glory of her squash-blossom hair and her handwoven dress. Omva held to her hand, planted both her
small moccasins on one of Vensi's, and swung in an arc as
wide as Vensi's arm would permit.

A white child tried to get Omva's attention and, failing,
shrieked in her ear: 'Hi! Hi! Hi, funny-face!'

Kaemana jumped at the shout and bent protectively
over her bowl. 'Do not mind, I beg of you!' she crooned to
it.

Vensi listened understandingly. A pot, though a 'made
being,' was nevertheless a being. A loud noise, it was said,
entered its unfinished self and might have to come out at
some future day, breaking its body to bits as it came. In her
own home, Kaemana would have been careful and quiet
when engaged in this delicate work.

'But what does it matter?' the Hopi woman said, laughing. 'This one will go to some staring *bohanna* who does not
know whether it is made well or ill, and if it does sing aloud
and break itself, little do I care. Few of these whites know
good work from bad.'

'Hasteen Clah,' Nuva contributed, tossing his head in
the direction of the hogan next door, 'he says that same
thing.'

Vensi looked shyly at the Navajo smith, Mr. Left Hand.
He sat at his door with his crude forge, while his wife, beside him, threw her yarn swiftly through the threads of her
loom. Hasteen Clah fashioned beads like raindrops and
like blossoms, and bracelets and rings that flowed together
around settings of skyblue stones.

Nuva chuckled. 'A *bohanna* looks at his handwrought
silver and she asks its price. "How muchee thisee ringee?"
she says. And Clah, he says, "Five dollars: pure silver,
good hard turquoise." And the *bohanna*, she squeals like a
clubbed rabbit: "Eeeee! Lookee, lookee! Heap much finer

work and more stones, only two dollars!" And she shows
him the ring she is wearing, and it is this kind of real Indian
jewelry that is made by *bohanna* machinery, a hundred at a
time; and the turquoise — pffff!'

Nuva imitated the loud-voiced white woman so well that
his listeners could all see her and her pudgy beringed fingers.
Kaemana and Lahpoo and their children shook with laughter, and the grandfather cackled high. Father and Mother
came running down the ladder to learn what was so funny.

'They are an outlandish people,' Father agreed, the
amusement-lines deepening around his eyes and mouth as
he surveyed the gay, mad confusion around him. 'I have
heard a word that they seem to love above all others: civ-il-
iz-ation. This, then, must be civ-il-iz-ation. And well do
they name the place "Whirls Fair." . . . Nuva, he tells me
that the word "whirls" means to spin like a top. Certainly
the fair spins, and the people spin, until one's head grows
dizzy with the spinning.'

'Have they no homes?' Lahpoo complained mildly,
finishing a katchina arm with his deft knife. 'Have they no
friends who would give them shelter, that they must walk
and stare all the day long?'

'And so queer-looking!' Kaemana marveled, like her
husband keeping on with her work. The thin walls of her
bowl quivered under her sure shaping. 'They are of every
color and size; they have blue eyes and brown, cow-colored
hair and yellow and white and black; and the women all
with such long legs.'

'Indians, whatever the tribe,' Vensi murmured to Nuva,
'all are of brown skin and black hair. Kaemana is right: they
match better. See yonder Seminoles. And those Indians
from Alaska ——'

From where they were standing they could see these and
others, for around the Hopi house were tepees and hogans
and cedar houses with totem-pole doors, and the palm-

thatched shelter where the Seminole woman sewed together
countless strips of colored cloth lightning-fast on a machine,
to make her rainbow dresses.

From the nearest tepee a young girl in beaded buckskin
waved a gay hand. Vensi enjoyed looking at her, she was so
exactly like the Indians on calendars and postcards: but
when Vensi shyly waved in response, a boy stuck his head
through the door-flap, smiling at Vensi, and then strode out
and stood by his sister's side. Vensi turned her back and
studiously watched Kaemana's swift fingers.

All the rest of that day Nuva sulked; and when dark came
he rolled himself up for the night without a word to anyone.

'What has troubled our son?' Mother inquired.

'Ask your daughter,' he growled. 'Ask her if it is fitting
that she let the Sioux Indian boy grin at her as he does.'

Vensi gaped at her mother. 'What Sioux Indian boy?'
she asked blankly; and then, remembering, 'Oh — the tall
handsome one with the many heads?'

At that Nuva sat bolt upright. 'You see! It is not
enough to let him look at her: she has been looking at him,
also. If you are not careful, she will be marrying him and
going off with him and his sisters to wherever it is that they
live.'

Father and Mother laughed aloud at his outburst, but
Vensi went pale with wrath.

'Marry!' she stuttered. 'I don't intend to marry for
years and years. Indeed, I wish I need never marry at all.'

She went back to the subject next day when she and
Mother were a little while alone. Mother was making up
Vensi's squash-blossom headdress, and it took time, be-
cause Vensi's hair had not grown far out of its little-girl bob.
It was still too short to be done up easily.

'Mother,' Vensi said, 'there are so few boys in our village
that are of the proper clan and phratry for me. And of
those who are, there is not one I like. Wiki — I would rather

die than marry Wiki! Why can't I stay unmarried, like Tawahonsi and her sister?'

'In all Middle Village they are the only grown women un-married,' Mother objected, brushing and brushing over the wooden squash-blossom frames.

'Sometimes,' Vensi said rebelliously, 'I think it is better to be like the whites, and not so afraid to be your own self, different from the others around you.'

'We are not afraid, exactly,' said Mother, 'we are —— But I know what you mean: we are much bound by custom; and much by what the rest of the village will say.'

'If Nuva were not my foster-brother,' Vensi murmured hesitantly — 'I am so used to Nuva. And I — I like him. I'd rather marry nobody, I think; but if I must marry somebody, he would be better than anybody else.'

'A foster-brother is not a blood-brother' — Mother spoke slowly, and her hands moved more slowly at their task, as if they were helping her think — 'And Nuva's mother was not of the same clan as yours, that much I have learned. Yours was of Sky Clan and his of Bear ... It would make it very good,' she added, happiness running like a laugh through her words and quickening her brush, 'to lose neither you nor the boy. But Honawu is set, and so also is Wiki's mother, which is worse ... But to have our Nuva come home after his marriage, instead of being lost to us in the home of another —!'

For such, of course, was the Hopi custom; the young hus-band became henceforth a part of his wife's mother's house-hold.

'But perhaps Nuva would not wish it,' Vensi thought sud-denly aloud. 'Perhaps he does not like me very well ——'

'Perhaps he does not yet know how well,' Mother con-ceded. 'But I notice he seldom calls you sister any more, and that means something.'

'Shhh!' begged Vensi; for Nuva's frowning black eyes appeared at the top of the ladder.

Close upon his heels came the young Sioux, three of them.
The girls exclaimed over the Hopi room, using many pretty
words, as *bohannas* did. The only Indian things about them
seemed to be their clothes and their name: Wildhorse. Alex,
Annie, and Edna Wildhorse. Most of their school years they
had spent with white boys and girls, and their English differed from *bohanna* English only in accent and tone. For
them it had been a lark to dress up in old Sioux attire and
spend a few weeks here with their grandparents.

And of course it was easy for them to mingle with the
whites at the exhibits and amusements of the fair. They
had come to ask Nuva and Vensi to go with them on an ex-
pedition.

Nuva's black hair quivered with unwillingness as he
interpreted their invitation to Father and Mother; and in
his black glare there was no friendliness.

'You would like to go with them, daughter?' Mother
asked Vensi.

Since the first night at Whirls Fair Vensi had entertained
a secret frightened wish to mount one of those animal
images and ride round and round to the blare of music. She
had longed even to swing up and over on the great upright
wheel. This was her opportunity. She moistened her lips
and whispered, 'Yes.'

'And you do not wish to, son?' Father asked with laughter deep in his throat. It was not Hopi custom to urge children against their wish.

Nuva flashed a suspicious glance at Father's smooth
face where the laughter was hidden, and a burning black
glance at Vensi — a reproachful glance. In a stifled voice he
said, 'I go also.'

When the group emerged from the Indian Village, Vensi
felt as if all eyes were focused on her costume and hair. The
silence of her moccasins shouted aloud. *Bohanna* shoes,
with heels to click on the sidewalks, would have been

quieter, she thought. However, the three young Sioux and
Nuva relieved her of some of the glances; and fresh marvels
were opening rapidly before her eyes.

The merry-go-round was as exciting as she had expected.
She rode a baby elephant that galumphed up and down as
it circled; and Nuva chose a giraffe immediately behind her,
while the young Sioux had horses and a lion. Alex rose in
his stirrups, whooping, and seized the silver ring as the
animals whirled past it; so he had a free ride and grandly
bought a second ride for his sisters and the young Hopis.
The Ferris Wheel also was a fearful joy; and after it came
other adventures that Vensi had not dreamed of: the Loop-
the-Loop, which left her gasping, the toboggan, and the
House of Laughter. Even Vensi chuckled aloud when she
first met her own reflection, in all her familiar regalia, gone
suddenly twice as broad as it was long.

While she and Nuva enjoyed the amusements, Alex and
his sisters seemed to be enjoying Nuva and Vensi. Nuva's
gloom blackened again when he caught their laughing gaze
upon him.

'They think they know so much. *Queevy*, proud,' he
growled in Hopi. 'I've noticed a person always does feel
big and wise when he is with someone smaller and — and
stupider.'

His temper sweetened when the five tried their luck at
shooting the wooden animals that moved in endless procession across an open booth. He was by far the best shot of all.

First he won a large doll with protruding eyes and feathers
in her hair. This he said he would take home to Omva —
'but it will give her bad dreams, maybeso.' Next he won a
big chiffon handkerchief. 'Mother will tie this around her
neck,' he said with satisfaction, folding it carefully into his
pocket. And his final prize was a wrist-watch with a leather
strap. 'Ridge-watch,' Nuva muttered, looking at it with
respect, and he handed it to Vensi.

'What was that you called it?' Edna asked impishly.

'Ridge-watch?' Nuva's answer was a question.

Edna exploded into a giggle which she tried to hide by coughing.

Alex came to his sister's aid. 'Here we are, in sight of the north entrance of the Fair,' he said hastily. 'What do you say we go "off the Reservation" and out into the big, big city? Like to, Vensi?'

Vensi shrank back and whispered, 'I don't know.' These Indians who were yet not Indians, and who laughed at Nuva and at her, even while they seemed to admire her — these Wildhorses confused her.

'Wouldn't you like a look at the things of our own people, Nuva?' Alex put the question to the boy, but his eyes stayed with the flushed Vensi.

'Things of our own people?' Nuva asked suspiciously.

'Yes. In that great big building down the street a piece, they've got images of the different tribes, and handicraft, and all sorts of old treasures — things that our old people certainly wouldn't have let the whites lay eyes on.'

Slowly, half unwillingly, Nuva and Vensi allowed themselves to be led along through the Fair entrance and on down the street to the imposing mass of the building Alex had pointed out.

There Nuva stopped. 'National Museum': those were the words carved above the stately façade.

'This is the place of the *bohanna* in the house-on-wheels,' he said in Hopi. 'I don't like,' he added in English.

So stubborn was his tone that the five might have turned away; might never have entered that portal. Accident and the prankishness of Alex decided otherwise.

A group of sightseers on their way to the museum paused to stare at the young Indians. Before the others could guess his intention, Alex seized the crude doll that Nuva carried under one arm, and set up a singsong shout:

'Doll for sale!' he chanted, doing a jerky dance with the doll held up before him. 'Hop-eye Indian doll for sale. Genuine doll belonging to genuine Hop-eye. Real feathers in its war-bonnet. Real war-paint on its face! Real cheap to the right party!'

Edna and Annie clung together, laughing helplessly; but after one incredulous glance at Alex, Vensi hurried ahead. She would have been glad to go anywhere that would separate her from this wild boy, so that people would not think that she was acquainted with him. The museum was the nearest hiding-place, and into the museum she darted, with Nuva close behind her.

VENSI and Nuva were scarcely through the door before Alex
and his sisters scurried in after them.

'Isn't he the limit?' Annie murmured, flushed and bright-
eyed. 'You never can tell what he's going to do next. But
it's all over now; don't look so embarrassed.'

Alex, his face pulled straight but secret laughter always
in his eyes, held out a dollar bill to Nuva. 'I hope you don't
mind,' he said. 'I didn't think it would sell so quick.'

Nuva pocketed the money, grinning a little himself. 'It
was ugly doll,' he said. 'You call it Hop-Eye, like the
whites, but I think that doll being Pop-Eye, no?'

Since they were inside the place, with its unpleasant as-
sociations, Nuva and Vensi timidly followed the young
Wildhorses to the Indian rooms. These proved a wonder-
land. Their only flaws were Alex's laughter and Nuva's
sulky spells and the *bohannas* who found five living Indians
more entertaining than relics of their past.

Vensi soon forgot the whites. She edged along the cases,

which resembled Lomavoya's showcases at home, looking at
baskets and pottery and arrowheads that other tribes had
made, like and unlike those she was used to. She stood
spell-bound before the great cases whereIndian groups were
displayed, life-sized figures in proper costume, with settings
of dugout canoes, tepees, wickiups, long-houses: figures so
lifelike that Vensi thought she could see their garments lift
with their breathing.

As directly as possible Alex and his sisters led the way to
the Sioux room. Its walls were lined with photographs and
paintings of former chiefs, some of them noble-looking men,
some plainly crafty and cruel. Vensi lingered longest over
the garments, the women's buckskin tunics and skirts and
moccasins all richly beaded.

'I think perhaps you'd like to be a Sioux girl,' said Edna,
the more mischievous of the sisters, tossing back the braids
she was unused to wearing. 'How would it be if you came
along home with us?'

Vensi blushed, and Alex laughed, and Nuva stared at a
stone club in a beaded case, his eyes so fierce that Alex's
laugh exploded into a snort.

'You look as if you'd grab that club and use it if you
could,' he said. 'You don't want your sister to be a Sioux, is
that it?'

'She is Hopi,' Nuva said with icy dignity, 'and it gets
toward dark and we must go home.'

Vensi looked at him from under her lashes, half pleased,
half anxious. Nuva could be so difficult when his wrath was
roused.

'Good gracious,' Edna protested, 'it isn't late. It's just
this cloudy weather. I shouldn't wonder if we were in for a
thunderstorm again.'

'Let's see what time it is!' Alex exclaimed, and he leaned
over to look at Vensi's wrist. 'Jeepers! Who'd have thought
it! It's twelve o'clock by the ridge-watch. Better let me
wind and set it, Miss Vensi.'

Hastily Vensi dragged the watch over her hand and gave it to him, and hurried on into the next room, where she thankfully immersed herself in study of the houses and totem poles and strange handwork of the Tlingits and Haidas. Nuva stalked behind them all. Glancing back she could see that he was keeping an eye on Alex and the watch, and presently he strode up and handed it to her, set and ticking.

'Now we go home,' he said.

'But look!' Vensi urged breathlessly. 'Cliff-dwellers. I want to see,' and once more the scowling Nuva trailed over the threshold after her.

Inside the room he forgot his smoldering annoyance. He even talked, though to the Sioux girls rather than to their brother, who stood by and listened with his lurking smile. In the relics of their ancestors, the cliff-dwellers, Nuva and Vensi found countless traces of their own present.

'Our women, they still using these brooms that are bunches of grass, tied tight,' Nuva told the girls. 'And still using rough flat baskets like those for storing things. And those round things, they like the whorls on our spinning-sticks; and these grind-stones — no different from what our mother using this day ——'

Vensi was peering through the archway into another room. 'Come, let us show them these,' she said in Hopi to her foster-brother. 'This is the Hopi room — all Hopi.'

'Good,' he answered; 'then maybe those girls will find out that it would be nice to come home with us and be Hopis.'

'You would maybe like one of them to do that?' Vensi inquired soberly.

Nuva glared at her so crossly that she laughed. 'My brother, he think maybeso you like to see these Hopi things, so maybe you want to be Hopi girls.' she said demurely, and led the way in.

She was proud of the display, and it pieced together for her the fragments of Hopi history she had always known. One case showed how the cliff-dwellers, driven from their more northerly homes by drought, had spread down through the old Province of Tusayan, long before it had been claimed by any whites, and when the ungrazed land was fertile: how first they had hung numberless of their apartment houses in such canyons as de Chelly; how later they had sought the open prairies, where the women built the tiny stone and adobe houses which belonged to them rather than to their husbands; and how the men planted and tended the crops.

It showed how warlike hunting Indians had harassed them, swooping down to steal their corn, their children, their wives; and how gradually the peace-loving ones had joined forces for self-defense, building their houses together on the sides of the mesas as they had done before in the cliffs — daily Vensi had passed the ruins of one of these old villages, Secuvi, near Corn Rock. Then, gradually, they had climbed higher for protection, until now these hundreds of years their villages had capped the mesas.

Suddenly Vensi's mouth rounded into a silent cry of delight, for she had found a model of Middle Village itself, and at its crest the House on Top. Her voice became quite audible in her excitement.

'Only,' she said seriously, 'they having our house not quite right. The ladder from below is too much this way — And see this chimneypot. When I clearing it I slip; and this is where I hang, with the rabbit-stick broken through the adobe.' She turned her hand, showing the scars of that adventure still red.

'But the very highest house of the village!' Annie squealed.

'Maybe that's why she's such a tiptop girl,' Alex put in jauntily.

'I think now we seeing plenty too much,' Nuva said with cold finality. 'I go back to Whirls Fair.'

'But ——' Vensi was trying to think of an argument which might soften him, when suddenly her eyes widened on an exhibit of modern basketry. 'Nuva!' she exclaimed. 'Look over in that glass case: is not that one of Mother's own baskets?'

Unwillingly he looked, as if suspecting a trick to detain him. '*Antsa*, truly,' he conceded, 'the large storage basket with the eagles.'

His glance moved on and he spoke with sharp astonishment. 'Vensi! Only see! In yonder case the stone lion-dog —— Is it not very like —?'

He did not complete the sentence. Neither of them was supposed to have seen the stone lion-dog that had stood among the Old, Precious Things in that dark chamber beneath their living-room.

Vensi looked, and went closer, and stood staring, staring at the fetish and at other objects ranged around it. *Bohannas* swirled unnoticed around the pair of young Indians in their bright clothing. As if she were sleepwalking, Vensi threaded through the throng until she stood pressed against the glass.

'The lion-dog,' she stammered to Nuva, close beside her — 'I did not think there would be anywhere another stone lion-dog with one eye of cannel coal and one of turquoise. Yet this has, truly, one blue eye and one black.'

Nuva said huskily: 'I never told anyone; but when I was too young to understand fully the wrong, I crept in where the Precious Things were, and took the lion-dog into my hands. My hands were too small, or maybe the gods were really angry. Anyway, the lion-dog fell from my grasp, and when I picked it up, the tip was gone from the tail.'

Vensi could hardly make her eyes move to the tail of the stone beast before them.

The tip was missing.

She moistened her lips. 'Those lightning-sticks, do you think?' she asked. 'And this old, old mask? And — surely there is no other *tiponi* like that; no other clan head would have quite the same insignia.'

Nuva was gazing at another and taller case that stood beyond this one. 'The blanket wrapped around — something,' he said in a choked voice. 'It looks like a blanket that our father wove. You do not see two patterns like that one.'

They slipped round the display of fetishes and worship objects and stood before this other. 'It is the very blanket,' Vensi whispered. 'Do you see that line of red in the near corner? Father let me weave it in, for a spirit path, I think.'

'But that blanket was wrapped around Tawamana's father when he died, and it was buried with him beyond Corn Rock,' Nuva argued as if to an unreasonable child. 'It couldn't be here and there at the same time, could it?'

Edna came around the corner of the other case. 'Why, what's wrong with you two?' she exclaimed. 'First you run off and we can't find you, and now you look as if you'd seen a ghost.'

'Ghost?' Nuva asked strangely, straightening up from where he had bent to look closer.

'Ghost — you know!' — Edna laughed, though she still regarded them curiously — 'The spirit of the dead — hanging around graveyards and all that.'

'What I see,' Nuva said gravely in Hopi, 'is not the spirit of the dead, but the dead himself. This is the body of Tawamana's father, Vensi. See the turquoise in his ear, like a turtle?'

To the Sioux girls and boy he explained: 'I seeing — what you call it? Skeleton? Mummy? — of Hopi man we knew well.'

The three gathered around them, exclaiming and staring,

while Nuva and Vensi moistened dry lips and tried not to
show their shock. Other partly mummified bodies lay in
the case, wrapped in blankets and decked with silver and
turquoise. Vensi studied them with burning eyes. How
many might be their friends, even their kin?

Nuva asked slowly, 'Would there be any way we know
who bring this things here?'

Alex said: 'The card just says, "From near Middle Village, Hopi country, Arizona." I suppose you could ask an
attendant. He might know whether there was any way to
find out.'

Vensi laid a trembling hand on Nuva's arm. 'No,' she
whispered. 'Let us go quickly away and forget what we
have seen here. It frightens me, Nuvayesva.'

Yes, it was too strange, too unearthly. That they should
stand here, hundreds of long miles from Middle Village and
all things Hopi, and that suddenly in the midst of the great
city of the whites a part of their own desert should enfold
them — this was like witchcraft. Perhaps it was witchcraft.

Nuva looked at Vensi, and looked at Alex, with his laughter always hidden in his eyelids. He looked at the brisk
young man who was leading the flock of *bohannas* round
the museum, explaining the exhibits in a sure, fluent voice.
Nuva murmured: 'Maybe you are right. Maybe it would do
no good.'

But when his eyes met Vensi's with that pulled-down-
curtain blankness, she knew that he was baffled and uncertain. Through her own mind many thoughts went whirling
— she had been wrong: they must get at the root of this
mystery.

'No,' she said, her breath coming fast, 'it is better that
we ask. It is better that we find out.'

Together they followed the group of tourists, and in a
pause in the guide's flow of information, they pushed reso-
lutely up to him. To her own intense surprise it was Vensi

who was saying, 'Mister, can we pleass ask you a some-things?'

The young man looked curiously at the slim frightened face between the satin black wheels of hair, at the slim Indian boy, like a flame in his orange shirt; and the *bohannas* wheeled toward the two as if on pivots.

'Why, certainly, Miss,' said the guide.

Nuva took over. 'I wondering,' he said, clearing his throat, 'could we know who bring those thing' — he swung his head toward the cases they had just left — 'from our vil-lage, Middle Village of the Hopi mesas?'

'You mean what persons sold them, or gave them?' the guide asked.

'Yess, I think so.'

The young man considered. 'There's a director in charge of such things' — he jerked a vague thumb toward another quarter of the building — 'but he's on vacation, on a cruise, so you couldn't reach him right now. And we couldn't go into it ourselves. But if you'd write to him, maybe he could tell you something about it. Or maybe not.'

'Where to would we write it?' Nuva asked directly.

The guide took a card from his pocket and held it against a case while he wrote a name and address. Nuva eyed it with a keen black flash and pocketed it.

'He won't be back there for another two weeks or more,' the guide reminded them.

'Thank you,' whispered Vensi, all her voice drained from her again by excitement.

Silently the two marched out of the museum; not until they were on the street again did they even notice their com-panions.

Alex vented his amazement in a long whistle. 'Well, I must say!' he declared, thrusting his hands into his buck-skin pockets and surveying the Hopis. 'You certainly did get all het up all of a sudden.'

'Better we don't tell nobody nothing about this,' Nuva responded stolidly. 'Not till we writing this letter.' He patted his shirt-pocket.

'Nohow!' Alex agreed with a twinkle. 'Put her here, pard,' and he shook Nuva's hand with vigor.

They went on toward the Indian Village. On their way the young Wildhorses insisted on stopping and having their pictures taken together by one of the Fair photographers, standing possessively beside a painted airplane, as if about to climb into the cockpit. Even Nuva submitted, though as if not fully conscious. His whole mind was engaged with the problem of finding a place where he could buy a writing-tablet and a stamped envelope.

For days Nuva and Vensi labored over their letter. Whenever they could snatch minutes free from observation they wrote and erased and consulted and wrote again. At last Nuva, whose penmanship was beautiful, copied the result with the greatest care. He kept his words sitting squarely on the blue lines of the paper — like snowbirds on a fence-wire — each a perfect little drawing in itself.

Then they put the letter away, since this museum chief would not be home to receive it for a while. Every day they took it out and re-read it, to see if it put their case as well as possible. They read it with mingled fear and wonder: fear lest their English might have cheated them, as it so often did, making them a laughing-stock; and wonder that they two could have done anything so fine and lofty.

Would it be possible, the letter asked, to know who had send or gave to Museem that stone line-dog, one turqoys eye, from Middle Village? Also the man in the cheif blanket with turtel in ear, from same place? Also manny other thing from Hopi village? And please oblidge and sent reply to Nuvayesva Yoki, Second Mesa. Arizona.

That letter was more than a letter: it might be a tool with which they could dig themselves out of a dark imprisonment. For if the *bohanna* in the house-on-wheels had brought those things to the Museum, then the people were right and he was an evil man, stealing from the dead — good though his thick yellow crackers had tasted. What was more to the point, if the *bohanna* had taken them, it would be plain that the gods had no hand in the matter, and Father and Mother would stand clear of all blame. Then how doubly good it would be to go home again, into their own place.

For one reason and another, the desire of all the Family was turning strongly toward the mesas; but it was a desire that proved hard to fulfill. Father had thought one month the duration of his engagement at Whirls Fair. The man in charge of the Indian Village said two. It was strange how many misunderstandings could creep into any agreement between Indians, speaking one language well and another poorly, and *bohannas*, speaking the other well and the one not at all.

Father explained that they must get home to harvest the early corn and pick and dry the early peaches. The man in charge snapped that what he'd pay Father would more than make up for his piffling corn and peaches.

Father, sitting on the floor finishing a blanket, tried patiently to explain, though such matters were hard to catch in words: Peaches and corn were peaches and corn, while

money was only pieces of metal. Hopis were too little used
to it; it slipped through their fingers and left behind nothing
to fill stomachs or cover backs. Little was left now of the
thirty-five dollars which had been paid the Family in ad-
vance. For one thing, there had been that amazingly costly
milk. Eight dollars had gone for milk alone.

The man in charge seemed hardly to hear Father, whose
reasoning sifted through his slick white mind without stick-
ing. He took from his pocket a paper which, without dignity,
he waved before Father's nose. At the bottom of the paper
stood an inky thumbprint, and beside the thumbprint the
words, 'Yoki, his mark.'

Yes, Father remembered signing, but it was for a month
he signed, he insisted. It was for two months he signed, the
man in charge countered, so that the Family would get
home with only two weeks of school missed by the boy and
girl.

'One month,' Father persisted.

'Two months,' declared the *bohanna* crossly; 'and if you
go home sooner, you can just pay your own food bills on the
way, and all your other expenses; and you'll forfeit the bal-
ance of your first month's pay, besides.'

The weather had proved hard on the desert Indians.
Yesterday a cold, wet wind had blown all day, chilling them
to the bone; today had dawned as hot and moist as a Navajo
sweat hogan. Discomfort and worry about the crops sat
heavy on the parents, while the young ones were pricked by
the hope and uncertainty of their secret.

'No other way?' Father asked patiently.

Again the man in charge shook the contract under
Father's nose. 'Not a thing on earth but sickness,' he
snorted, and stamped down the stairs.

Vensi sat weaving an eagle, whose difficult beak and tail-
feathers should have taken her whole attention; but
through her mind was running the question: Sickness?

Sickness? Couldn't she eat something that would make
her sick but not too sick? Couldn't she stand out in the
rain, next time there was rain, and be soaked through and
take cold?

But she didn't know of any food that made her sick, and
she had been drenched a hundred times without hurt. And,
besides, sickness, throughout her years, had come to spell
such a misery of pain and fever and chanting medicine-
men and crowds of sympathetic and annoying neighbors,
that she flinched from hunting up a sickness on purpose.

And then, when ten days of the second month had crawled
by, the matter was taken out of the Family's hands. The
heat of late August thickened around them, lay heavy upon
them, stifled their nights. It was thick heat, like a steamy
blanket, not like the thin bright heat at home, conquered by
adobe walls or the shadow of a tree or even of a clump of
sagebrush.

A doctor, making a routine visit on all the Indians in the
village, had persuaded Mother to spread down a blanket
and let the *tiposhoya* lie on it, naked except for his diaper.
Already his thin skin, unprotected by coloring-matter, was
red with heat-rash, and he was not eating well. Even the
cool, sharp days did not strengthen him, and now, as the
heat pressed closer, unrelieved for days and nights, whatever he did eat disagreed with him.

The Family grew anxious. Here where no healing herbs
grew, and where field nurse and Mission-Mary were beyond
the miles, with their *bohanna* varieties of wisdom and medicine, Mother did not know what to do for the little one.
The Family took turns holding him and walking with him,
but he cried more and more, not the full-bodied cry of the
past two months, but the fretful mew they had known at
first.

Again the doctor came. He looked at the limp little body,
like a flower uprooted, and put a glass tube under the little

arm while he pressed an inquiring finger on the blue wrist. Through the young people he explained to Mother a change in feeding, and then he held a pad against his knee and wrote a prescription. He tore it off and handed it to Nuva, who looked at it blankly.

'Take it to the drugstore and they will put up the medicine I've written down,' the doctor said.

Nuva took the prescription to the drugstore and waited a long time, wishing he could walk around and look at all the remarkable things crowded into the one building, but afraid if he left his seat near the prescription alcove he might lose his medicine when it came.

At last a clerk stood at the counter and called out a mysterious string of syllables unlike the former 'Smiths' and 'Browns.' With interest Nuva watched his mouth, opening so wide under the overhang of his nose. After he had called the syllables two or three times without result, the clerk beckoned to Nuva and held out the bottle, marked Nuvayesva Yoki. Nuva stared at the words and wondered how the clerk could have made them sound so strange. Then he took the bottle and started away.

'Just one minute, son,' said the clerk. 'A dollar, *if* you please.'

Nuva had to leave the medicine and go home after the dollar. Never before had the Family been asked to pay for medicine.

And still the boy-baby drooped and wailed. And again the doctor was summoned.

'The root of the matter,' he told them, 'is this heat. My advice to you is to go home, and go home quickly — And in an air-conditioned car,' he added.

The Family, too much worried to feel triumphant, made all haste to depart. The first thing Nuva and Vensi did was to read the letter for the final time, seal it with care and compare its address with that on the museum card. Into one of the green mailboxes which had been pointed out to them they stuck that letter, with a sense of emptiness in having it gone from their hands, to fail or to succeed.

Mother and Vensi had to finish a few baskets that had been ordered, and while they were weaving Father and Nuva managed to do a little shopping. Nuva had carved tops, and had made cows' heads and sheep's heads from a sackful of vertebrae he had brought along for the purpose; and of these trifles he had sold a great many for a few cents apiece. If he had had paints and paper, he said somberly to Vensi, he might have made real money with pictures, but now it was too late. So he bought a beaded buckskin vest he had set his heart on, seeing it in a curio store. And Father traded his best moccasins for a pair of oxfords, tan and brown, very stylish.

Mother and Vensi did not go shopping at all. Throughout the whole six weeks Vensi had hoped and feared to venture into the bewildering canyons of the city streets and into one of the trading-posts she had heard about, as big as the railroad station. There she had hoped to get a dress, or even two, and a pair of smart shoes. If she left the city without them, who knew whether she'd get them at all? As Father had said, money slid away like shelled beans running through the fingers. The doctor — the medicine — the milk ——

And always there was Father's debt to Honawu, waiting at home to leap upon them and empty their pockets.

Nuva was sure she could find dresses and shoes at the drugstore. 'In that drugstore they have everything on earth,' he said with conviction.

But Vensi had no time for shopping, and no heart for it, with the boy-baby growing so rapidly worse. As soon as the last basket had been handed over, they packed up and raced to the great station again, Alex going along to help them check their baggage and get aboard.

with wetness, he stepped hard on the accelerator and sent
the light truck bouncing and pitching over the rough road.
Going this way, he must cross an unbridged part of Oraibi
Wash.

The rain swept onward like a great gray curtain. They
could see it coming and feel it coming. First they breathed
washed air; then they smelled the pungence of wet sage
and other growing things; then the odor of water on hot
dust stung their nostrils, and the downpour was upon
them.

The Family huddled into their blankets and tucked the
tarpaulins tighter round the load of groceries, and enjoyed
the rain.

'Rain at Whirls Fair, it is entirely different,' Father
grunted with satisfaction.

'This is good, but the Wash will be running,' said John-
Jack. 'Three big rains since Snake Dance, and already
the washes are running a little.'

How could the *bohannas* say that the Snake Dance was
foolishness? Vensi asked herself, cuddling Omva closer
under her blanket, the little girl giggling with excitement
at the clean wetness splashing now and then on their faces.
Almost always till the Snake Dance there was drought.
Almost always after the Snake Dance — sometimes the
very day of its ending — there was rain. Of course, she
remembered, Miss McClung had an answer: she said that
the Snake Chief chose the time just before the rains would
begin anyway, and that that explained his success. Vensi's
mind seesawed between the Mission explanation and the
Hopi one.

But now she hoped that the gods would be moderate in
their response and not halt the truck this side of Oraibi
Wash. She had set her mind for the two days home by
train and for another two or three days to the Second Mesa
post-office. For those four or five days she could endure the

suspense that stretched her nerves tight like dry rawhide.
But delays would be almost too much to bear.

John-Jack was as anxious as the Family. Vensi could
almost see him prick up his ears as he neared the Wash.
Certainly there was a roar of waters, but it was a far roar,
muffled by distance. As one person the Family held its
breath while the truck thrust its muzzle downhill into the
Wash, plowed through the wet sand of the floor, and climbed
out again on the other side. A few minutes more, and they
would have had to camp on the bank till those distant
waters had raged by and subsided.

In another hour they caught the flash of their own silvery
windmill in the forenoon sun; and then they came in sight
of the ranch-house, small and dear, sitting waiting for
them in the sand. Father's brother's wife and children
came scurrying to meet them and help carry in their goods,
and John-Jack's muddy truck rattled away toward First
Mesa.

The women chattered fast that morning, and Father and
Nuva went out to find the men; and when noon came and
they all sat at ease on the earthen floor and ate the good
things spread before them, their talk began all over again.

No more sheep had been lost to the coyotes. No more
burros had trampled and destroyed the fields. Uncle had
thought the beans and late corn lost by drought, but the
rains had come in time so that they were making a fair
crop. The early corn was ready for gathering, and the
early peaches ready for picking.

'And the *tiposhoya*, he has grown to be a man!' the aunt
cried.

'And this Omva, she is no longer even a young lady,'
said the uncle.

'Omva *bas lolama* — very fine!' Omva declared solemnly
— 'Cute kid,' she added reminiscently, in English she
had heard at the Fair.

'It was all very grand, I suppose,' Aunt observed, at last remembering Whirls Fair. 'And the cities, are they really as big as people say? . . . No, I didn't think so,' she answered herself before anyone had time to answer her.

At that, Father and Mother, Nuva and Vensi, were all chattering together. Bigger! they told her. She would have to see it to guess. People with money to throw to the winds. Houses so big that it would take all the men and women on the mesa a year to lay the stones for one.

'And much rich food?' asked a cousin.

Nuva, his mouth newly filled with *somiviki*, nodded vigorously. 'But nothing,' he added when he had swallowed, 'so good as Hopi food: the poor *bohannas*!'

'And no place so good to live as our Hopi country,' Father put in, looking with supreme content at the sandy fields and at Second Mesa, bleak but beloved, over against the sky.

As soon as dinner was done, the Family went at the harvesting of the early corn, the sweet corn. Small though the stalks were, none of them taller than Vensi and most of them not so tall, the ears were fine and well filled. Usually the harvest was the occasion for a work-party, with friends and relations coming from the mesa and gathering and feasting. This year the crop was too small to warrant the larger picnic, but the two families had one of their own. For the first time in their lives, this year, Nuva and Vensi found the fun over-long. It seemed as if it would stretch out forever, keeping them away from the Second Mesa post-office.

'But we may as well enjoy the sweet corn,' Nuva warned Vensi, 'for who knows? Perhaps we shall wait days and weeks for the museum chief's letter. Perhaps he will never answer at all . . . though the Sioux boy, when I asked him, did say that our letter should have reached him next day, if he had come home to where he lived, because it was a town next door to the Whirls Fair city. And if he got our letter next day and answered it at once, why, then!' — Nuva's dark face scowled and laughed with eagerness — 'But don't expect it right away, Vensi!' and he shook his head at her in elderly warning as he went back to his task.

He was helping Uncle dig the roasting-pit and build the fire in it and pile in stones when it had burned down to good coals. Cleverly, too, Uncle made openings for flues, which would keep the low fire fanned throughout the night.

Into this pit was heaped the harvested corn, all in its silky-green husks, and earth was shoveled in on top of it. There it steamed away all night long. Uncle and the cousins had caught fat young prairie dogs, and the women covered them with clean clay and put them to bake, too, so when morning came a rich feast was spread. The scent of strong coffee and succulent meat filled the air, and the most delectable of odors steamed up from the opened corn-pit.

They all ate and ate, and even when they had eaten themselves full, they had not made a dent in that rich, steaming pile.

Now the remaining ears must have the husks stripped back and knotted together, and must be hung where they could dry evenly and be ready for winter use. It was a tasty morsel when the snow was whirling around the high mesa: an ear of corn popped into a kettle of boiling water and cooked tender. The wind might be shrieking in at the peepholes as the Family were eating that corn from the cob, but they could imagine themselves in their fields again, the summer sun strong and hot upon their backs.

Always Vensi's back grew tired and her fingers grew sore, over this task, but usually she liked it. Today it was monotonous, and she almost envied Omva, who was entirely happy in the food and companionship of the moment.

Omva trotted around her elders, her mouth ringed with

corn kernels and her hands busy with husks and silk, or dragging her kid, which had almost outgrown her. Once, to be sure, Vensi became aware that the little girl was quiet, and looked over to see her squatting motionless, still holding her corn playthings, her great eyes fixed on the ground near her.

Vensi's glance darted to their point of focus. That point was a half-cone of spangled scales, from the top of which extended a flattened head, with beady eyes agleam.

Before the rattlesnake could strike, Vensi's foot scuffed along the ground and sent a shower of sand over the reptile. And before it could rid its lidless eyes of the blinding sand, she grasped it by the tail and flung it far out away from workers and ranch-house.

'She is not so much of a coward, your girl,' Uncle said approvingly. 'I thought this was the one who trembled when a person spoke to her. . . . I thought this was the one called the Whispering Girl.'

'Before persons, yes,' Father admitted. 'Before persons she is not brave. But otherwise ——'

Father smiled at Vensi, and she felt that this long-drawn interval had after all held a glory.

As SOON as the sweet-corn harvest was cared for, the two
families stowed themselves and their possessions into the
wagon and left fields and ranch-house behind them until
November should bring the harvest of bright-colored field
corn and of fat yellow beans.

Uncle and Nuva started across country to Second Mesa,
herding the flocks, and Father drove to First Mesa and
Lomavoya's store.

'We are as shabby,' Vensi murmured to Mother, 'as
when we left Lomavoya's to start to Whirls Fair.'

'But then we had no money and now we have — a little,'
Mother reminded her, and as she said it she pulled the buckskin pouch out of her belt, where she had tucked it, securely
wrapped in a rag. She handed it up to Father. Together he
and she had decided that her belt was the safest place for
the precious cash; but now, with so little time remaining, it
did not seem likely that any harm could befall it.

'To know that you have money, it makes you feel better inside yourself,' Vensi admitted. 'And the jewelry makes you feel better, too. But I certainly had wished that we should go back to Middle Village wearing new dresses from the city.'

Father wore his black sateen shirt; the black had run into the white pipings only a little, and the silver shells from belt to collar made a fine showing. Father could, besides, enter the village in the magnificence of his sport oxfords, though they were too painful to be long endured. Mother and Vensi, on the other hand, had only their faded old dresses, grown no newer. They would have felt funny in their Hopi costumes, besides feeling hot; save for a few old women on the nearer mesas, and others in the far villages like Hotevilla, no one wore Hopi dresses any more except to the ceremonies. Before the women clambered out of the wagon, then, Mother and Vensi spread their summer shawls over themselves and Vensi pulled down her best bracelet so that it would show well.

Inside the store, the first thing Vensi looked at was the bolt of red-and-white plaid gingham: the piece she had picked for her prize in the Fourth of July race — if she had dared run the race, and if she had won. There was no more than a yard left.

Clucking regretfully, Mother had Lomavoya's clerk thump down the other bolts on the counter. For herself she chose a green print with small orange flowers, and then she waited for Vensi to choose hers.

But Vensi edged closer and whispered that she would rather, if Mother did not mind, order a dress from the catalogue when she sent for her shoes and Nuva for his jeans trousers and blue shirts — since there was not enough of the red and white plaid left.

Secretly Vensi was glad it was gone. She knew what style of dress Mother would make: the style the first field nurse had taught her when she was a little girl. It would have a snug waistband and a plain waist gathered to the top of it and a full skirt gathered to the bottom of it, and plain wristbands for the full sleeves. In the catalogue was a dress with a flaring skirt and short sleeves puffing out deliciously. Ever since the catalogue came, Vensi had kept the corner of that page folded over.

Mother looked doubtfully from Vensi to the bolts of print and gingham. 'Maybeso you would better choose another piece while we are sure of it,' she counseled, speaking under her breath. 'You never can tell ——'

Vensi said, 'Yes, but I would rather have the dress in the book. And — oh, Mother, I want to get home!'

Mother let it go at that.

By the time Father had paid for the supplies purchased the month before, and for the pawned hard-goods which the trader had let them take out, and for Mother's dress-goods and Karo and coffee, the pouch had grown thin. Mother took it from Father's hand, and weighed it in her own, and, sighing, tucked it into her belt again.

What remained was less than they had feared. If they used even a few dollars to pacify Honawu, they would have no more than enough for a scanty outfit apiece for Nuva and Vensi: one outfit, with no changes.

The bills paid, the trader opened a complimentary box of soda crackers and two cans of tomatoes. The Family and Aunt and the cousins sat on the floor or leaned against a counter and ate, slowly and with relish. After all, what was gone was gone, Father's expression seemed to say, and here were tomatoes, never to be despised. But for once Vensi was glad there were only two cans and a small box of crackers.

Lomavoya watched them benevolently, leaning back against his shelves with his thumbs hooked into his plump belt. Suddenly he began to laugh, his strong white teeth flashing below his small mustache.

'That Honawu,' he said, as if just remembering, 'he was very mad when he heard you were going to Whirls Fair.'

'And how did he find it out?' Father asked.

'It seems he heard a whisper of it when you drove away from Second Mesa, and quick he came to learn for himself ... You had not told me it was a secret matter.'

'But what affair was it of Honawu's?' Father queried, while Aunt's bright, curious eyes turned from one to the other, pleased at the prospect of a story.

'He said you should not go away without paying him that old debt,' Lomavoya said with some amusement. 'He said he would get the Council of Middle Village and the Village Chief, and even Mongwi himself, to stop you and put you in jail ... It is not good to be so angry,' he added more soberly.

Vensi stopped eating to listen. As always, the name 'Honawu' made a sickness at her stomach.

'Why should he be so mad?' Father wondered aloud, swallowing a luscious mouthful of tomato from the can. 'Well he knew that I had no money to pay him. If I went to Whirls Fair I might have money' — he shrugged humorously — 'or I might not; otherwise none, till Washindon takes part of my sheep again.'

'He wanted to go to Whirls Fair himself, maybeso,' Mother whispered on a drawn-in breath.

'And yet,' Father objected, 'that does not explain such an anger.' He frowned. It was a deep puzzle.

'He has told me something he is angry with you about,' Lomavoya said in a tone that withdrew a little. 'But I do not believe it.' He looked searchingly at Father and Mother, and nodded as if satisfied with what he saw. 'I do not think the gods have more cause to be angry with you than with many others. Honawu's own woman has also gone to the Mission for the sewing: I know that. And who of us does not go there at Christmas time when so many gifts are given?'

Father and Mother and Aunt made small grunts of assent. Vensi was thinking that Lomavoya did not often go, but that always he sent treats: a whole bag of Christmas candy, ruffled and fluted and striped; or apples; or oranges.

Lomavoya leaned across the counter and spoke softly, though at the moment there were no other customers. 'The Old, Precious Things of the Clan, my friend, is it true what that one says about them?'

Aunt's mouth popped open. Father and Mother looked at each other and at the floor and at Lomavoya. 'Half-true,' Father answered huskily. 'But of where they now stand, or how this has come to pass, we know nothing.'

Vensi choked on a cracker and hid her cough and her hot face in her hands, her heart pounding. How astounded Father and Mother would be if they knew what she and Nuva had seen! More than ever she longed to hasten home, to learn whether a letter had come, and, if it had, what it might tell. She could see herself stepping into the small post-office and standing at its window, not needing to say anything. She could see the letter sliding under the wicket, while the postmistress looked at her in surprise that she, Vensi, should get a letter.

Lomavoya had more to say, leaning on his hands, which were blue and white with rings. 'Honawu is about to put up a new building on Second Mesa. Yes, and at Middle Village it is. There will be a work-party. Tomorrow, I think; so you are just in time.'

'A new building? What new building?' Father asked alertly, poising one of the cans at his lips again.

'A trading-post. He has bought the stock from Tayma, in Shungopavi. Honawu is to be a rival of mine,' Lomavoya said, and laughed. He was so much bigger than all competitors that he did not mind them any more than a burro minds a few flies.

'Where does he get money to buy the stock?' Father queried.

Lomavoya shrugged and grimaced. 'Who can say? He does boast that he will have enough sheep to supply all the mutton he needs for some time: your sheep, brother, that he says you owe him on that old gambling debt he is always talking about.'

Father pushed back the tomato can as if his appetite had turned against him. 'If Washindon takes a part of my flock and Honawu the rest ——' he said.

'But maybeso if we pay some of the debt in money,' Mother breathed, her eyes flickering down toward the slight bulge in her belt — 'Sheep are better for us.'

Vensi hid a small gasp, like the gasp of one who has been plunged into unexpected cold water. That dress with the puff sleeves. Those shoes.

A darker thought seized her, a thought so black as to blot out the loss of dress and shoes. With Honawu thus inexplicably angry, would he not soon succeed in persuading the Village Council that Father and Mother were not fit and able parents? Unless the letter ——

Lomavoya sighed and said: 'But it seems that we Hopis are not the only ones on this earth who are poor and hungry. Have you seen?'

He thrust out his hand toward a pasteboard box with a slit in its top. Fastened to it was a poster bearing picture and printing.

The Family and Aunt and the cousins studied the picture. It showed small children with swollen stomachs and legs and arms as thin as the *tiposhoya's* had been: legs uselessly crossed because powerless to bear up even the small weight of those large-headed, large-stomached bodies. Vensi's eyes jumped, startled, to the printed words.

'"Chinese re-lief,"' she sounded them out in a whisper. '"One dol-lar — feeds — one — starv-ing — child — for — a month."'

The many pairs of eyes sharpened in their scrutiny and then pivoted slowly to Lomavoya.

'Yes,' he said, 'your girl is a scholar. It seems to be true. The Mission-Marys say so, also Mongwi and the Water-Witch.'

'Where?' Vensi whispered the question to Mother, and Mother shifted it, with her querying eyes, to the trader. 'And couldn't we give them corn and a mutton?'

'On the other side of the world they are,' Lomavoya answered, with an indulgent smile for Vensi. 'Beyond the Underworld, they say.'

'But why is it so with them?' Father asked. 'Did they have drought? Or was the winter too heavy?'

'It was not drought nor cold,' said Lomavoya, his kind face pitying the children on the poster. 'Their people fight, and wherever there is fighting there is also hunger.' He lifted the box, its poster-top swaying. From inside came a feeble jingle of coin. 'We are giving what we can,' he said, 'but you know how little we have. If we could send sheep or corn — but it is too far away.'

Within herself Vensi was saying, *Grandmother says when Corn Rock crumbled and the famine was, her mother took Grandmother's sister to the Rock and sold her to the Mexicans. And Grandmother's mother carried the sister on her back, though the child was nearly a woman, because she was so weak from hunger that her legs were useless. Like those in the picture.* 'Why, we ourselves are fat!' Vensi whispered to Mother.

They both looked from those sunken baby faces to Omva's, round and smooth. Omva's wrists had a crease around them, and her fingers a shadow of dimples at their bases.

'But we cannot give. There are too many of us here to feed,' Mother said sorrowfully. 'Look. This one also.' She drew the cover from the boy-baby's cradle.

The boy-baby regarded the trader with startled solemnity for a moment, and then, making sure that he was being smiled at, he lifted one little lip and grinned wider and wider until his face was one delicious toothless mouth set in a pucker of dimples.

'*Lolama!*' Lomavoya cried, clicking his tongue at the baby. 'You have done well with him. No, I know we cannot all give to these China babies.'

But Father had taken out his penknife, and with his chin tucked down into his neck and his tongue caught between his teeth, he was snipping the threads with which Mother had sewn the silver shells to the black sateen shirt. One — two — three — four — five. The top one he left, his shirt bulging open below it, and handed the other gleaming shells to the trader.

'How much?' he asked.

'The same as you paid for them,' Lomavoya answered. 'Fifty cents, a dollar, a dollar-fifty, two, two-fifty,' he counted.

Reaching sidewise to his impressive cash register, he sent the drawer jingling open and scooped out the required coins. Into Father's hand he clinked them, and Father dropped them, one by one, through the narrow slit in the pasteboard box.

Vensi's heart was swelling larger and larger and she hugged Omva tight. Think if it were Omva as hungry as that! Ordinary half-hunger was one thing, keeping always a little gnawing in the stomach. That was normal and to be expected. But this hunger —! And these babies were not *bohannas* (in which case Vensi would have found their suffering a shade more endurable): they looked like Hopi babies. Vensi thought that they probably were Hopi babies. Doubtless their forefathers had gone downward from the Underworld instead of upward, as her forefathers had done.

She looked at her rings and bracelets. The plain silver
bracelet would bring little; and one ring had a soft stone
that was darkening to watery green. But her other bracelet
—— The turquoises were not large, but they were the best
stones, hard and clear and sky-bright. She had always been
proud of that bracelet. She turned her wrist sidewise
through its narrow opening, and silently held it out to
Lomavoya.

As silently Lomavoya took three dollars from the cash
drawer and handed them over the counter to her. She
could hardly see the poster as she fumbled the big silver
disks through the slit. Three! She was feeding a Chinese
baby for three months, she, Vensi.

Lomavoya was scooping more silver from the drawer:
five more dollars and a half-dollar. One by one he dropped
these, also, into the Chinese Relief box, while the Family
and Aunt and the cousins watched him questioningly.

'Why is this?' Father asked.

'I have said it,' the trader explained. 'For each dollar the
others put in the box, I put one to match.'

Not only three months, then; not only five and a half; no.
Between them they and Lomavoya would keep one of those
babies from hunger for — Vensi counted her fingers swiftly
under cover of her shawl — eleven months; or eleven of the
babies for one month.

Lomavoya reached under the counter and brought out
five large safety-pins. Father pinned up his gaping shirt-
front with them, and the two men grinned at each other.

'After all,' said Father, 'these hold it just as tight.'

Determined-looking clouds were piling up behind Second
Mesa and spreading cool shadows on the plains as the
Family left the trading-post. The mules pricked up their
ears and clipped off the miles eagerly, smelling rain and
smelling home. Their hoofs beat no faster a tattoo than
Vensi's heart. *Home — letter? — Home — letter?* her heart

THE CRIER

AT LENGTH the talk of the elders was done. Father shook
the reins over the mules' backs and touched them with his
whip, and the wagon creaked up the hill toward the village.
In the back sat Vensi, clutching the letter and murmuring,
'Yes,' and 'No,' and 'Fine!' to Omva's chatter without
hearing what it was that either she or the child had said.

Uncle and Nuva turned the flood of slow-moving white and black sheep and goats up the mesa road behind the wagon, and Nuva ran ahead of the woolly mass to murmur to Vensi. Later, Vensi lifted Omva out of the lumbering wagon, as if to gather for her a *chemona* flower blooming white in its mass of blue-green leaves; and then she called breathlessly to Nuva, using phrases the others would not be able to make head nor tail of: 'Could you have believed if you had not read it in black and white words?' — 'Stone mouths — stone mouths, too, Vensi!'

Sometimes, though, they could talk unheard, and in those scattered moments Nuva and Vensi sketched their plan of action.

First, it would be better to tell Father and Mother nothing as yet. If in the village the Family should hear allusions, friendly or unfriendly, to the disappearance of the Old, Precious Things, it would be better for Father and Mother to meet those allusions with empty faces, not knowing what their children had learned.

As soon as possible Nuva must see the Agent. By great good fortune, Mongwi might this minute be in Middle Village; or he might come tomorrow; but such luck was unlikely. Probably Nuva must make excuse to go down to the Mission and telephone him, or must borrow a horse and ride over to the Canyon. Nuva preferred the latter plan, for thoughts tangled one like spider webs, when one tried to send them along those *bohanna* wires, and especially thoughts so new and surprising as those which the letter had brought.

'Why should we not instead tell Miss McClung this story?' Vensi suggested. 'We could safely ask her what it is best for us to do. Her words are always straight.'

Nuva slowly shook his black mane, the thin curve of his lips pinched straight and his eyes fierce with thought. Mechanically he lifted Omva up and set her on an old stone wall. The wall was the corner of an abandoned sheep corral, but different from the side walls: of a firmer masonry. It was all that was left of the Franciscan church which a Hopi mob had destroyed at the time of the Pueblo Indian uprisings of 1680. Not far away was the place where the padre had been burned. Yes, the padre had been burned, and the Hopi priests had rejoiced because, they said, they had killed God and the Virgin Mary, and had washed away the People's baptism in sacred corn meal. Nuva's glance and Vensi's turned toward the friar's place of martyrdom as the boy spoke.

'It is true her words are straight,' he acknowledged, 'but this affair of ours is a matter of Hopi religion, and it is best not to carry it to one of the *bohanna* religion. You understand? Always they see only the darkness of our faith. Like this' — he nodded toward the corner of the old church. 'Even to Mongwi I am sorry to have to tell it, since he is white. Much better if we could manage by ourselves; but we are too young to know what is wise to do. And if we tell the parents, I am afraid of what would happen. They would be angry at what this letter has said. Can you imagine how angry?'

'*Okiway*,' Vensi breathed, an excitement of fear shaking the word: 'Angry indeed; and such anger cannot deal well with what we have to deal with. But still, I am afraid of other things. I am afraid something bad will happen before you can get to Mongwi.'

'Do not fear,' Nuva said in the gentle, fatherly voice that always amused and touched her. 'I can maybe get away tomorrow.'

'Even tomorrow,' Vensi protested, 'might be too late.'

She climbed into the wagon again with Omva, and Nuva followed the sheep slowly past the old corral and its corner stones steeped in blood and black memories.

When the Family reached the Top they found the mesa,

below their house and a little to one side of it, black with
people. Already Honawu's work-party was in progress,
laying up the walls of his new trading-post in Hopi masonry,
the flattish stones laid one on another with their edges
showing. Beside Lenmana's had stood a ruinous old house,
long deserted because its family had died out. It had now
been pulled down, and Honawu was building on its site.

He stood directing the heavy work, and he twisted his
head to look over his shoulder at the Family as they came.
From the shelter of her lashes Vensi watched his face, trying to read the expression there. Its flitting shadows seemed
to escape Father and Mother, who showed only surprise
at his cordiality.

'*Antsa*, truly,' he called in a patronizing voice, 'here are
our world-walkers home again, and rich, I suppose likely'
— his eyes flicked Father's safety-pins.

Mildly Father replied, even while a surge of cold fear
shook Vensi. Father spoke uncertainly, as if he were thinking that his old enemy might have had a change of heart
while the Family were away.

Vensi had so long planned how she would cover as much
as possible of her poverty when they re-entered the village,
that now she automatically spread her cashmere shawl wide
over her patches. But she hardly noticed the curious
glances of Polemana, her mind was so filled with the unexpected turn of affairs which the letter brought about.
Nuva, too, though he presently swaggered up from the
sheep corrals in his beaded Sioux vest, seemed only half-
conscious of his own splendor: as if his strut were machinery
which he had set in motion long before and had not bothered
to stop.

As soon as they had dumped their belongings inside the
House on Top, the Family went to their peach trees. The
location of their small orchard was such that summer
visited it early and brought the fruit early to maturity

The Family must pick the ripest this afternoon. The coming rainstorm would damage it.

'And tomorrow,' Father said slowly, 'we shall spend much of our time at the work-party. If Honawu is disposed to be friendly, we must certainly do our share toward mending the old break.' Father frowned, his eyes clouded with thought.

Nuva also frowned. It might be hard to get away, even long enough to telephone, if they were to pack the whole of tomorrow full of peaches and building stones.

An unpleasant surprise greeted them when they reached their trees. Certainly other pickers had been before them; the crop which remained was the smallest the Family had had in years.

'*Okiway!*' Mother whispered, looking at the half-stripped trees.

'What was to be was to be,' muttered Father.

Without more words about it, the Family set to work, picking fast, spurred on by the billowing clouds. Scarcely had they got their fruit into the protection of their peach hut — one of a row of shelters there on the ledge of the mesa — when big raindrops began to burst around them. By the time they reached the Top, the work-party was running to cover, shouting and shrieking with laughter.

'Our brothers the snakes have certainly carried our prayers to the gods this year!' Father called genially to one of the workers who was sheltering himself in a curve of newly built wall.

'But we did not ask for floods!' the man objected, laughing.

'It may be that the gods are really angry,' put in Tayma, the Shungopavi man who had sold Honawu his stock of goods. 'Something I have heard about their taking away their belongings from a household in this village, because the household had angered them.'

At that, Father went silently into his house. Vensi,
following Mother with Omva cuddled under her shawl,
flashed a quick glance toward Honawu, down in his own
doorway. Honawu's eyes, more than ever like black
beetles, slid toward Tayma when Tayma spoke, and
Honawu's mouth was cruel as a closed trap.

Inside the House on Top, Mother went about caring
for the *tiposhoya* and making a meal, her face such a mask
of unhappiness that Vensi longed to read her the letter and
ask her: 'Mother, what will it mean? And what shall we do
with it?' *But yet a little while, my mother*, her thoughts
said. *Yet a very little while.*

Throughout half the night it stormed. The lightning
whitened the room with swift light and blackened it with
swift dark, and the thunder crashed and rattled and
rumbled away at length into distant mutterings which
let sleep come.

Next day the sun rose in a clear sky and on a mesa washed
clean. The villages had no sewerage system and no garbage-
collectors. A storm like this one, beating upon the adobe
roofs and upon the stone streets and upon the horse corrals,
swept away the filth and the rubbish with a million urgent
brooms; and the hot sun of morning steamed and burned
the village almost to sweetness. Even the shallow reservoir,
carved from the living rock centuries ago, had in these
August storms been washed and refilled, and now smelled
clean.

It was a great day for work, and the Family was among
the busiest on the mesa, two working with the peaches
and two at Honawu's building.

'We must still show ourselves friendly,' Father had said
as they sat at breakfast that morning. 'Maybeso it was
chance that Tayma spoke as he did.'

'If only such speech does not rouse the friends of Honawu
and Mutz to violence,' Mother murmured, holding the

tiposhoya's bottle for him with one hand while she ate with the other.

'Ours are not a violent people,' Father chided her, 'and now, with Mongwi only an hour away by automobile, even the most un-Hopi of Hopis do not easily turn to violence. Washindon does not permit.'

'But all the same,' said Mother, pulling the bottle from the boy-baby's mouth and letting the nipple fill with air again before she replaced it, 'all the same, I remember what happened to Twoitsi only last year; and then, also, Mongwi was but an hour distant by automobile. It is not hard, if you wish to rid yourself of someone, to have that someone slip and fall from the mesa top ——'

'But why should they wish to be rid of me?' Father inquired reasonably. '*Antsa*, truly, Honawu would take my flocks; he would try to get Mongwi to take away my fields and give them to others; he would try to influence the Village Council and even Mongwi to take from us our children; he would marry our daughter to that slack-spirited Wiki if he could; but all this he could do without killing me. If the new Mongwi is soft and anxious to please the more powerful Hopis — which I think he is not — then it would be very easy. But even though Mongwi prove hard to handle, I see no cause for anyone to kill me.'

Nuva shot a quick glance at Vensi: a glance black and bright with both fear and knowledge.

'Father,' Nuva ventured, 'why cannot I go down to the Mission-Mary's and telephone Mongwi to come here?'

'Come here? Why should he come here?'

'We could tell him,' said Vensi, her voice thinning to its away-from-home whisper, 'that trouble threatens.'

Father shrugged. 'I cannot see that there is anything to telephone him about, Daughter. These are enemies of ours, that is all. They harass us as flies harass the mules; but that is ours to endure... No, Son, you stay here or

else help with the peaches: it is needful that we show ourselves friendly.'

That morning Vensi and Mother worked with the peaches
picked the day before, while Father and Nuva helped with
Honawu's walls. The women took Omva and the boy-baby
with them, and the boy-baby slept deeply in the clean air,
while Omva laved herself with ripe fruit, getting more on
her face and dress and hands than into her mouth.

Mother was quick and deft with the work, and Vensi's
skill was usually nothing to be ashamed of. She could break
a fruit apart with one twist of the wrist, and lay the peach
open side up to dry, working almost as swiftly as the older
women. Along the same flat stone ledge they all spread
their split fruit, where the sun beat down hotly and the
rock held the heat.

Today Vensi's fingers stumbled and she worked as if in
a dream. Her hands, as always, grew sticky and sore with
juice and fuzz, and the scent of the peaches rose heavily
in her nostrils. Usually she enjoyed it — out in the open,
with all the fruit she chose to eat and the companionable
chatter of the neighbors around her. Today she hated it:
it went on and on, dizzily; and she caught herself always
listening for reproach or unfriendliness in the chatter; always wondering, *How goes the work-party? Is more evil
talk simmering there?*

The women asked, curiously, about Whirls Fair, and
about the train, and whether meals were really cooked
upon it as it raced across the land. In their turn they told
about the new babies who had come, and about the people
who had died, and how hard it had been to find enough
rattlesnakes for the Snake Dance this year, and of the
outrageous manners of the *bohannas* who had come to
witness it.

Vensi's mind tried to brush away these troublesome
gnats of talk and return to her underlying anxiety: *How*

soon can we get in touch with Mongwi? Will it be soon enough?

When Tawamana began to talk, however, Vensi listened. She listened, not because Tawamana was saying anything of importance, but because the cheerful briskness of Tawamana's voice sounded forced.

She said that she found one of those *bohannas* in her piki room and another in her storeroom; yes, and without so much as a by-your-leave. No, she did not miss anything, but she was almost sure the one in the storeroom was carrying a picture-machine not much bigger than a watch, and she had a mind to call the Village Chief to deal with him, since picture-taking was not allowed on the mesa any more. But the worst of it, she said, was that she had a brood of baby chicks in the storeroom. She had set a dozen eggs and had had the good fortune to hatch six, and then the good fortune had been chased away by bad; for this *bohanna* was a man.

Mother cried, '*Okiway!* then I suppose your chicks died.' That was to be expected, for a man's coming into the place where they were kept was the worst of luck for them.

'Every single one!' Tawamana responded with gloomy satisfaction. 'A burro stepped on one, and two were caught in the rain, and two had a sickness, and Lenmana's youngest hugged the last of them ... Every single one dead inside a week.'

Yes, surely Tawamana's round kindly face looked worried; surely her talk was unnaturally fast and nervous, almost as if it kept step and broke step with Vensi's hurrying breath. Maybe she was trying to keep less friendly women from much speaking. If so, she was successful; she and the women's haste to finish the morning's task and get to the work-party before dinnertime.

Most of them helped Lenmana and her daughter with the cooking. By noon Lenmana's floor was covered with kettles of rich-smelling stew and with fresh corn and with baskets of peaches and hard little apples, and with watermelons the size of muskmelons, and with *potas* heaped with piki and freshly fried bread. There was a washboiler full of coffee, too, and all the sugar and canned milk anyone could wish.

First the men ate, the women serving them. Nuva sat cross-legged on the floor with other boys of his age, and when they had finished eating, Father beckoned him from across the room with a backward toss of his head. Vensi, slipping round like a shadow to help refill baskets and kettles, listened anxiously to what was said.

'Son,' said Father, 'you go now and pick peaches, and the rest of us will stay and help our neighbors.'

Vensi's heart dropped. Perhaps Father thought it safer to get the boy's quick temper away from provocation; but the Mission and its telephone were on the other side of the mesa from the peach trees. That was unfortunate, unless — she thought, her pulses racing again — unless Nuva meant to disobey Father, going down the trail instead of around the shoulder of the mesa.

Nuva looked at her meaningly as he went, but she could not tell whether the meaning was, 'I'll manage to telephone,' or, 'It will be safe to wait till tomorrow.'

With all her heart she hoped it was the former, for she did not feel that it was safe to wait, with the tension, the unfriendliness, thickening here in the milling throng of workers and idlers.

Was she imagining the threat of storm, her own nerves keyed too high? No, for now, at once, the first rumblings sounded.

Honawu looked after Nuva, his brow darkening. He is wishing, Vensi thought, that he had that strong, handsome boy for his son. Till Nuva was of marriage age he would be useful in this new trading-post, lifting heavy boxes which Honawu's frailty could not manage, and keeping accounts which were beyond Honawu's untutored knowledge. And when he was older — Vensi's heart jumped with anger at the thought — Honawu could marry him to his daughter Polemana and so keep him forever. But even more than wanting him for himself, Vensi thought again, Honawu wanted to take him away from Father and Mother.

Honawu's eyes turned from Nuva's erect black head to Vensi and Mother. Mother had such a kindly face, and so much of bright youth lingered in her hazel eyes, that her shabby dress made little difference. Lenmana, now, wore crisp new print like a flowered tent over her bigness, and her necklaces and bracelets clanked like harness. But Lenmana's close-set eyes and thin lips were almost lost in the fatness of her face; and any kindness they had ever held was lost with them.

Honawu's glance went on to Father. 'It is kind of you to help your neighbor,' he said. 'But that reminds me: Now that you have been to the Fair and have of course much money, you will want to settle the little debt you owe me. Of course I would not mention it,' he added silkily, 'if it were not for my new store. A new trader needs much money.' Honawu swelled with importance as he said it.

Father's face stiffened. Mother, across the room from him, made an almost imperceptible movement, and he spoke: 'It is impossible for me to pay you much till Washindon buys my sheep. My children need clothing for school, and we have had no time to work it out.'

'Well, then,' Honawu came back contemptuously, 'how if you and I were to have another game? — Your debt all paid if you win, and your sheep driven into my empty corral if you lose!'

Again Mother stirred convulsively, bending over the boy-baby's cradle to hide her agitation. It had been long since Father had been led into a game, but this time he paid no heed to her unspoken reminder. He looked around him at the listening people. Though their faces were impassive, he was so used to them that he could read even the blankness, Vensi knew; and certainly there was rebuke in the stolidity of some.

'*Antsa*, truly,' Father agreed wearily.

Straightway the two sat down against a wall that shielded them from the afternoon sun, and began a game with the soiled and broken cards Honawu pulled from his pocket. If it had been any of the other villages, Vensi thought wretchedly — if it had been any other of the whole six on First and Second Mesa — this could not have happened. Much as the Indian loved to gamble, such gaming had been outlawed in every village but Middle Village.

So the thought of their play sat heavy on Vensi as the women and girls ate. She could not do justice to her tin plate, heaped with good food. Things had come to a pretty pass when a mouthful of rich, meaty stew was practically nothing to her.

Now that the women were at leisure for an hour and could savor hominy and gossip together, there were some whose sliding eyes and veiled words were swift clouds and stabs of lightning to Mother and Vensi.

Omva and the *tiposhoya* were the only members of the Family who were completely at ease. The *tiposhoya* was propped up in his cradle against the wall, and looked round him with the haughty air common to young babies, except when someone saluted him, calling out 'Snowball!' or 'Aberaham!' and clucking or poking. Then his sober little face would open up in his own sunny grin, and sometimes he would crow ecstatically. And Omva ran in and out among the company, plumping herself confidently down beside this one or that one, getting bites of the different delicacies. Every one of the women and girls, and some

of the men and boys, must look at her Japanese doll, slung
securely in her flowered shawl; and most of them had to
measure how much she had grown during the summer.
To the little children the Hopi village was one big home,
where nobody could be unkind.

When the eating was done, the afternoon stretched like
a cord of wet buckskin, unbelievably long. The women
helped clear away food and dishes, and, since the roof had
been put on, some of them lent a hand with plastering.
Vensi busied herself with the care of the children, and
occasionally made an errand past the two players.

Her heart sank at the quiet triumph that shone like
oil on Honawu's face. And Nuva? Was he really picking
peaches, over on the shoulder of the mesa? Or was he at
this moment telephoning from the mission?

Even if Nuva was telephoning, could Mongwi do anything to help? Could he come to their aid in time?

Not if he were at the Canyon, for Wepo Wash ran between, high and angry from last night's storm. Vensi's
stomach was sick as she pictured what might happen if
Honawu won the game and ordered the sheep driven into
his own corral. Father was gentle, but his deep-held temper
could be violent when finally loosed.

The August sun dipped below the rim of the mesa. The
men stopped their work. From a housetop a voice called:
'Work-party again tomorrow. Everybody is invited.' It
was already 'crying-time,' and yet Nuva did not come,
either from the peach orchard or from the mission house.

'Hi-yah!'

Vensi jumped at Honawu's shout of triumph. Father,
getting stiffly to his feet, had gone gray-green.

'You, Wiki,' Honawu croaked, 'drive this our friend's
sheep from his corral to mine. Already his brother has
herded them up, for I have heard that broken bell of
his.'

Father laid a protesting hand on his tormentor's arm, but Honawu shook it off.

'What do you say, men of Middle Village?' he called to the villagers, lounging around the unfinished building. 'Now this one is trying to slip out of his bargain. Is he a good Hopi, would you think? There are few of you who do not know that the gods have shown their displeasure with this family. To those few perhaps it is time to say that the Old, Precious Things of the Clan, the things which his women was given to tend — these have disappeared.'

With a low murmur of anger, the men moved closer.

'Yes, and why did he not tell of the loss? Why but that he knew that he and his wife were guilty? He knew that they had wandered, in their thoughts if not in their deeds, from the Hopi religion.'

'When did these things vanish?' Tayma asked. 'Was it not while the *bohanna* in the house-on-wheels sat over yonder on the shoulder of the mesa, behind the trading-post? The white man who tempted the People to sell their treasures? Even worse, who tempted them to break into the sacred graves of their dead?'

At that suggestion, the angry murmur deepened. Vensi, watching with a fearful fascination, thought she understood Honawu's swift, remonstrant glance toward Tayma; but certainly Tayma did not understand. Indignantly he pushed on:

'We all know that someone led the *bohanna* to the old and secret chamber cut in the living rock of this mesa and painted by the Ancients themselves. We know that the *bohanna* profaned the sacred place with his picture-making — though we took from him his rolls of pictures. We know, too, that this man' — he indicated Father — 'stayed long in the house-on-wheels one day.'

'As to all that, what good in talking?' Honawu broke in impatiently. 'If our brother has sold the Precious

Things, it can never be surely known. They are lost to the People forever, and another link with the past is broken; but if it be true that the gods have taken them away because of the unworthiness of him and his family, then the anger of those gods may be softened by his punishment.'

Again the muttering deepened and swelled, like the hum of bees about to swarm. *Why did not Nuva come?*

'If we were to strip him of his children,' Honawu went on, licking his lips with anticipation, 'and take away the fine fields he has held too long already ... If in the division of the communal lands next year the Village Council should give him stony acres, far from water, to discipline his soul ...'

'We should tell Mongwi,' Tayma came in urgently and with the ring of sincerity. 'If your Village Council, your Village Chief, were to go to Mongwi in a body, not one or two or three as heretofore, and explain the evil here ——'

Vensi shoved the boy-baby's cradle into Mother's arms and slipped softly as a shadow up one ladder, up another. Her body was shaking like a bough of poplar leaves, and this thing she was setting out to do she could not do.

Running through the first room of the House on Top, she dragged from the pole of soft goods a large, dark blanket. This she wrapped about her deftly, hiding herself from chin to toes and swathing her head and face except for eyes and nose and mouth. Then, before her terror could quite unjoint her limbs and freeze her blood, she climbed the ladder to her own housetop.

For a moment she stood looking down from that highest peak of the village. She looked to the right, to the quarter where Nuva might appear if he were coming from the peach trees. He was not there. She looked to the left, where the trail bent up over the edge and into the village. He was not there. She looked out at the road, that deep nail-scratch, which led from First Mesa. Along its winding fled no car. She looked down upon the people of the work-party and despair held her.

Almost all the men of the village had clustered around Honawu's dwarfish figure. Only a few had ranged them-selves beside Father.

Vensi moistened her lips and cleared her throat and opened her mouth —— But, no, this thing she could not do.

'O men of Middle Village!' she cried in a wavering chant like the criers', but so small that the people could not have heard her through air less thin.

As it was, they heard, and their heads jerked up like the heads of the puppets in the Doll Dance. Father's eyes were round with amazement, so that she knew that he had recognized her. So also did Mother. Omva did not: Vensi could see her as she trotted busily around hunting for her big sister. There was no recognition in the other faces: little, whispering Vensi was the last person on earth from whom her neighbors would have expected any daring deed. Her own repute disguised her more completely than did her swathing blanket; and the knowledge gave her courage to go on.

'O men of Middle Village,' she repeated in a voice that cracked with strain, 'do you know where Honawu obtained the money which he has paid for Tayma's goods? And do you know what in very truth has happened to the Old, Precious Things of the House of Sivenka? Listen well and I will tell you, for I know. Verily, I have seen these things since they were snatched away from the place of their abode. Yes, I have seen them, and that not in a vision but with the eyes of the flesh.'

Vensi closed those eyes, so that she might not see more of the murderous rage that flared into Honawu's face. Her slight body swayed as if the breeze were shaking it, but she went on.

21.   THE FAMILY

SHE must go on, while Honawu was still held in a paralysis
of amazement. Before anyone could stop her she must get
her story told.

'Ask Honawu,' she called, in the measured chant of the
crier. 'Ask him when it was that he slipped into the House
on Top and took from it the Old, Precious Things. Ask him
when it was that he galloped with them to First Mesa and
sold them to the white man in the house-on-wheels — the
bohanna who was gathering treasure, by wrong or by right,
for the great museum in the East.'

The silence below Vensi was like a gasp. It was like
the intake of breath when one has been ducked in ice
water. The faces turned up toward her were blank with
shock.

'Ask him if that was why he wished to keep Yoki and his
Family from going to Whirls Fair — because it, too, was in
the East, and indeed in the very city of the museum, so that
Honawu feared Fa —— Yoki might happen upon that place
and upon the Old, Precious Things, and might then learn
the dangerous secret.'

She took a fresh breath. Very near had she come to saying 'Father'! She must be more careful. Her small voice piped on again, bird-clear and child-small.

'Did you see, O men of Middle Village, how this one searched Yoki with his eyes when Yoki returned yesterday to the mesa? Truly, he read in Yoki's face that he had not learned the dangerous secret. Therefore did Honawu make haste to blacken him even blacker in your sight. For if all were certain that Yoki's house was guilty of the loss of the clan treasure, would not Honawu's guilt be forever buried in that belief?'

On the highest wave-crest of the village Vensi stood, a little figure all alone. But a strange thing had happened to her. She was not afraid.

The throng below gaped up at her in complete silence — at her, Vensi, who had never willingly attracted anyone's attention. Her heart swelled with a sense of power. She plunged on:

'Ask Mutz, also. Ask him where he found the money for the hard goods that shines upon him. Ask him how came the skeletons of Hopi children in the glass cases at the city of the Whirls Fair for the whites to stare at. Ask him how did the father of Tawamana, three years dead, walk to that city with his blanket about him and the turtle turquoise in his ear? Ask him would he like to see a letter about those skeletons and those Old, Precious Things, written by one of the white chiefs of the museum himself?'

The frozen stare of Mutz, down below, further exhilarated Vensi, until her mind was to her a shining bubble, floating above her own head and flashing out strange new colors. She took breath for a new venture, but she was stopped by the first interruption to come from below. It came not from Honawu, nor yet from Mutz, but from Father.

'So this is the answer,' Father said into the tight stillness. 'You two have taken sacred things and have made a mock of them, and then you have laid the blame upon me and my woman.'

Father made no move toward Honawu and Mutz, nor did he raise his voice. All the hidden pain of years of small persecutions rang through his words like the low notes of a trumpet. Honawu settled back on his heels and crossed his arms on his breast. His glance flicked here and there among the people like a snake's tongue.

'You have taunted me with being over friendly to the whites,' Father went on. 'You have said that my family has walked white paths and earned the enmity of the gods, bringing ill-fortune to my village and to the People. You have looked sidewise at the children we have taken, because you said they were children of misfortune, harmful to the village. We have wondered why, then, you wished to take those children into your own homes, but now we understand. It is because you do not believe either in the gods of the whites nor in your own, and you are willing to buy and sell either. *Antsa*, verily, I say unto you' — Father squared his shoulders and raised a solemn hand — 'I have looked upon the white religion and I have asked myself whether it is not perhaps the Way that we should follow. A clean Way it is, with no ugliness in it. It is a Way that leads through the Light. This I say to you in truth and at last without fear. But I say also that I, Yoki, a little doubting the old gods of my people — I would have cut off this hand rather than secretly take the Old, Precious Things and give them, for money, to the white man.'

Now more than ever Vensi's mind floated clear and bright above her head. She looked out across the plain, where the buttes and mesas also floated, with the same lightness and color as the clouds that billowed above the setting sun. Bright clouds floated above her, bright clouds below her, and there she hung at the heart of a bright, beautiful world from which fear had for a little while fled.

And now when she no longer needed them, Nuva and Mongwi had come. Mongwi's car had turned the curve in

the trail and nosed up into the village. Unnoticed by any
but a few women and children at the fringes of the throng,
Mongwi and Nuva had got out together and stood listening
to the whole of Father's passionate avowal. With waves of
exultant feeling, Vensi saw that Nuva was rapidly inter-
preting Father's words to the Agent. That was a good
thing; but it was still better that the Family should have
taken care of this matter by themselves.

As yet the two had not seen her. When Father ceased
speaking she took up her chant anew, and the two new
heads jerked back with the rest.

Inspired by a growing conviction, she cried in Hopi and
interpreted in her halting English, saying: 'This man Yoki
is he whom Honawu and Mutz and their friends have
blackened throughout the years. Ask them why. He is the
man from whom Honawu has again and yet again won
money and silver and sheep. Why? Because Yoki played
with a straight heart and Honawu with a crooked. Crooked!
Crooked every game he has played. And this debt that he
has held so long, threatening Yoki with it, ask him if it was a
fair debt!'

While Vensi was putting the bold accusation into English,
she was watching its effect on the accused. Honawu set his
face like a stone and kept silence. Mongwi must see, Middle
Village must see, that this silence was confession.

Nuva's face gleamed up at his foster-sister and friend
with a clear admiration before it turned back toward the
milling and muttering crowd. Certainly the temper of that
crowd had changed. Restrained by the presence of Mongwi,
the people yet shot dark glances at the betrayers. Never
again, Vensi thought with a great uprush of joy, could
Honawu and Mutz lead them to believe ill of Father and
Mother. She would have liked to stay where she was,
watching the triumph of the Family, but she must seize this
moment when no one was observing her. Softly she stole

down the ladder from the roof. The concealing blanket she flung in at her own door, and sped downward to hide herself in the fringes of the throng.

There she stood, making herself small in a corner, when Mongwi walked with Father and Nuva toward the home ladder.

The men let their eyes slide past her, though Mongwi had to twist his mouth downward out of a quick smile. Mother said, not really looking at Vensi: 'Come, my daughter. Mongwi eats with us this night.'

Only Omva, with a squeal of delighted discovery, flung herself upon her big sister and clasped her about the knees.

With Omva on her shoulders, Vensi followed the rest of the Family up the two ladders and into the House on Top. She walked straight, eyes ahead, until she had passed from the sight of the silent people. But once inside the house, she felt her knees buckle, and she sat down abruptly on the floor, trying to act as if she had meant to sit. She was as tired as if she had raced up the trail from Corn Rock. Her heart jumped and her mouth was salty and dry and all the strings of her joints were untied.

Father looked down at her with sparkling eyes, and touched with his toe the blanket which she had dropped on the floor a few minutes earlier. 'After all, she is not wholly without courage, that one,' he told the Agent, and indicated Vensi with his head.

Mongwi came and held out his hand to her, and she laid a clammy little paw in his. He looked at her curiously.

'You once told me that there were other things besides fatness,' he said, giving her hand a pat with his other. 'You were very right.'

Mother went into the storeroom and brought out the shiny bulk of the new mail-order catalogue. She handed it to Vensi.

'Pick out your school dresses, daughter. Two, I think.

And the plaid jacket and the shoes and stockings. And Nuva his trousers and shoes and a jacket with sheepskin inside against the keen winds of winter. We will send for them at once, to be in time for school ... Sit still: you look as pale as one long sick. And no wonder, doing so bold a deed.' Her words scolded gently, but her smile was warm and tender.

Vensi sat with Omva tumbling over her knees and hanging to her shoulders. Nuva brought her his best pencil, and sat beside her, helping pick out, while Mother quickened the fire and stirred the simmering stew and sat down beside the cradle to give the boy-baby his bottle. Quickly Vensi leafed through the fresh, inky-smelling pages. A dress with delicious puffed sleeves stood in the new catalogue also.

With his little-man strut, Mongwi strode to the peephole above the grinding-bin and gazed out at the wide-flung view; strode back, laying an appreciative hand on the mellow plaster, on the water-jar with its time-faded patterning. He nodded approval at the painting of Corn Rock on the wall. He leaned over the catalogue to see what the young people were selecting, and nodded approval also of the page, the page of artists' colors and pencils and paper. Supper was soon ready, and Mongwi nodded approval of supper.

Father offered him his choice of a stool — two inches high and eight inches wide — and the fluffiest sheepskin, and Mongwi folded his legs awkwardly on the sheepskin. For him there was also a plate and a knife, a fork and a spoon.

The stew was good, and the fresh corn was good; the bread was delectable in its crackling crust of fried bubbles; the melons were sweet and cool. And there was plenty for everyone.

For a while Nuva sat quite still, staring through the peephole; but presently he roused himself and ate until he had to lean back against the wall and, grinning, loosen his fancy belt one hole. Boys could always eat. As for Vensi, under

her faded gingham she had no stomach, no stomach whatever. She had nothing but happiness; and she thought probably Father and Mother were feeling as she was.

None of them talked much, though Father did say, medi-
tatively, 'But only a few of all Hopis being mean people.'

Mongwi nodded understandingly.

Mongwi ate, and then sat smoking with Father: wild
tobacco, rolled in fine corn husks, he smoked, as Father did.
At last he clambered down the ladders; and, much as she
had learned to like Mongwi, Vensi was glad when he went.
The Family was again alone together.

Now the village was still, except for a few comfortable
sounds that came up from below: of children laughing inside
other houses; of late sheep-bells clanking up to the corrals.
The room was dim with evening shadows. Through the
peephole above the grinding-bin shone a keen little moon,
bright as a pendant of new silver in the cool blue sky. The
plain was darkening, and a red spark emerged from under
the mesa and followed a yellow glow along the winding nail-
scratch of road. Those would be tail-light and headlight of
Mongwi's car.

Vensi looked across the room. It was too shadowy to be
seen with clearness, but it was beautiful.

Mother said, 'This winter, I think, we can buy oil for the
lamps.'

Nuva said nothing. Father said nothing. He lay back on
the floor with his arms under his head and Omva climbed
him as if he were a mesa.

Vensi yawned contentedly. She was almost too sleepy,
suddenly, to help clear away the food, but she would not
waste any of this hour in sleep. For this was a good hour.
It was the best.

THE END

GLOSSARY

Antsa (ahn'-chah): verily, or truly.

Banda (band'-a): headband.

Bas (bahss): very.

Bohanna (boh-han'-na): white person. A corruption of *Amelakahan*, American.

Chemona (chee-moh'-na): flower of nightshade family.

Concho (conch'-o): silver shell ornament: Spanish, not Hopi, word.

Eskwalli (es'-kwah-lee): Thank you (woman's form).

Katchina (kah-chee'-na): a spirit or force of growth; a lesser deity.

Lolama (loh'-la-ma): good, fine, beautiful.

Manta (man'-ta): woman's mantle.

Mongwi (mohng'-wee): chief.

Nuvayesva (Noo'-vah-yes'-vah): Snow.

Nuvensi (Noo'-ven-see): Snowflower or Snowflake.

Okiway (oh'-kee-wy' [long *y*]): Too bad! Alas!

Omva (Ohm'-vah): Cloud.

Pikami (pee-kah'-mee): corn-meal pudding.

Piki (pee'-kee): paper bread.

Quaequae (kwhy-kwhy'): Thank you: man's form of expression.

Queevy (quee'-vy): proud.

Somiviki (soh-mee'-vee-kee): corn-mush marbles tied in husk to cook.

Tiponi (tee'-poh-nee): insignia of clan head: scepter.

Tiposhoya (tee-pos'-hoy-a [hard *s*]): little baby.

Tiposie (tee-pos'-ie): [hard *s*]): baby.